THE
SOUL BROTHERS
AND SISTER LOU

THE SOUL BROTHERS AND SISTER LOU

KRISTIN HUNTER

CHARLES SCRIBNER'S SONS   NEW YORK

75-135

2031

For JOHN,
who hasn't read this,
but doesn't have to.

THE
SOUL BROTHERS
AND SISTER LOU

ONE

LOURETTA HAWKINS WAS WALKING HOME FROM SCHOOL VERY slowly. Every day she did this, taking the long way home with very short steps, because she was in no hurry to get there.

It was not that Louretta didn't love her Momma and her seven brothers and sisters. It was just that she wanted a place—even a corner of a room—that was all her own, so she could have her own friends over to visit. But with nine of them—no, ten—in a five-room house, there were no corners to spare.

Louretta wished for the nine-hundredth-and-ninetieth time that she had someplace to go between school and suppertime. Someplace where she could talk, and have fun, and be with her friends. But in Southside, the part of the city where she lived, there was no place to be with your friends except the sidewalks and alleys.

As she walked along, dragging her feet very slowly because she was almost home, she sang her favorite new song, the one that was on all the jukeboxes and radio programs, *My Devotion*:

You vanished like mist on the ocean,
You fled like the glow from the stars.
There only remains my devotion
As proof of the love that was ours. . . .

Louretta knew all of the popular songs and sang them often, in a strong, clear voice that was somewhere between alto and contralto with a little catch in it, a little break resembling a sob. She didn't think there was anything unusual about her singing. Most of the other kids her age also knew all of the songs, and most of them could sing, and did.

Almost at the alley behind her house, she stopped. It was too early to go home. Besides, the boys were singing in the alley. Every afternoon in the spring, summer and fall, they gathered under the tree in the alley—sometimes to fight, and sometimes to share a bottle of wine bought by an older boy and tell stories, but mostly to sing. And when you heard them singing, you forgot that they were in an alley full of weeds and garbage cans and skinny, hungry cats.

Ah-oo, ah-oo, ah-oo-oo-wee,
Baby, how you thrill me . . .

It was beautiful, with Ulysses' deep bass and Frank's and David's mellow baritones in close harmony in the background, while Jethro's high, sweet tenor rang out clearly, singing the melody. Louretta leaned against the wall out of sight and listened. She wouldn't be able to hear them much longer. It was October, and when the cold weather came the boys wouldn't be able to meet in the alley any longer. They would have no place to go.

Once she had asked the boys why they didn't join the high school glee club. Jethro had screwed up his impish copper-colored face in a frown and said, "Oh, baby, that glee club is a drag. They make you sing *Sweet Adeline* and *Jeannie with the Light Brown Hair* and all that kind of lame, square stuff. That drags me, baby. That ain't my bag."

He had balled up his fists and begun dancing on his toes like a boxer, playfully tapping big, easygoing Ulysses on the shoulder, trying to start a fight. "Hit me, man," he kept saying. "I dare you. Come on, hit me." All the teen-age boys in Southside could fight, but Jethro, in spite of his small, wiry build, was the toughest and the one who won most often. Sometimes Louretta thought he fought all the time so that no one would dare to say anything about his high, girlish tenor voice. No one did. Except that when he stopped fighting and started singing, it was beautiful.

> I'm just a poor ship at sea,
> And the waves are drowning me . . .

Now Ulysses was carrying the melody, and Jethro and the others were singing the "ooh-wee" part, moaning in the background. They really sounded like the sea.

Boys have all the fun, Louretta thought angrily. No one minded if boys spent all their time in streets and alleys. When girls did the same thing, people said they were bad. But where else was a girl supposed to go?

She knew what Momma would say: "Go to church." Louretta did; she sang in the choir at the Methodist Tabernacle on Sundays, and even played the piano when the regular church pianist, Mrs. Morgan, couldn't come. But she couldn't be happy, like Momma, going to church every other night in the week. She needed something else to do.

Standing there listening, she wanted to go in the alley and join the boys. They might tease her and call her Red, which always made her angry, because her hair was *not* red, it was dark brown. But they might be glad to see her. They might even let her sing with them.

"Don't you let me catch you fooling around with those bad boys in the back streets and alleys," Momma always said. "You see what happened to Arneatha. If the same thing happened to you, it would kill me."

Louretta didn't really think a thing like that would kill her mother. She was too big and too strong and too wise for that. When Arneatha's baby, Cora Lee, was born, she'd just taken it calmly and started raising it like one of her own. Of course, it was supposed to be a bad thing that had happened to Arneatha. It was especially sad because Arneatha hadn't even been in love with James Lee Walters; she'd just hung around his house after school because she had no other place to go. Still, with Momma taking care of the baby, Arneatha was free to get dressed up and go out on dates and have as much fun as she ever had.

Of course Arneatha had been forced to drop out of school. One thing Louretta was sure of was that *she* would finish school. She glanced down at her battered pile of books. English was her favorite subject; the teacher, Miss Hodges, always praised the way Louretta recited poetry. She had gotten A's in English and music and history last term, and B's in all her other subjects except math. Everyone said Louretta was smart. She'd even skipped the seventh

4

grade, so that now she was the youngest one in the tenth grade at Southern High. Fourteen. She would go on; she would graduate, and maybe after that she would work for a while and save up enough money to go to college, though college was such a grand and faraway idea that she never even talked about it at home.

Momma wouldn't understand Louretta's wanting to go to college because she'd never gone herself and didn't believe anyone should try to rise *too* high. "I never went beyond the eighth grade, but I'm smart enough to raise all of you," was what Momma always said when any of them tried to show off. Even her big brother William, who usually sided with Louretta, said college was only necessary for boys. But one thing was certain: Louretta intended to finish high school, no matter what any of them said.

It was hard, though. Arneatha was the one who had cut classes and hung around boys' houses and gotten into trouble and had to drop out of school. Louretta was the one who went to school every day and did her homework and got good marks and never even let a boy kiss her. But the results seemed to be just the opposite of what they should be. Arneatha was the one who had pretty brown skin, and pretty black eyes and hair, and pretty clothes, and flocks of boy friends who wanted to marry her. And in the evenings when Momma went out to church and Arneatha went out on dates, Louretta was the one who had to stay home and do the dishes and mind the children and give them their baths and put them to bed, all in addition to her homework. It seemed that Arneatha would always be Momma's favorite, no matter what she did, while no matter what Louretta did, she would always come second.

Louretta thought she might as well do whatever she wanted, because it would never even cause Momma to get a gray hair. Though sometimes, late at night, when Momma was rocking Cora Lee to sleep, her face would get a sad, tired look, as if she were wondering if the same thing would happen to Cora Lee when *she* was sixteen. Sometimes it didn't seem to matter what Louretta did. But if Momma's precious only grandchild ever had a baby without a husband, that would *really* kill her, Louretta thought.

She was jolted out of her thoughts by the sight of a patrol car sliding up to the curb at the corner and a big, red-faced man in uniform getting out. It was Officer Lafferty, and he was coming this way—heading, with his big, swaggering steps, straight for the alley.

In school they taught you that the policeman was your friend. Louretta and all the other Southside pupils smiled wisely whenever a teacher said this, because they knew better. They knew that all policemen were not *their* friends, even if they might be the friends of children on the other side of town, and that some policemen, like Officer Lafferty, were their worst enemies. Officer Lafferty's favorite sport was to catch groups of Southside boys in out-of-the-way places like vacant buildings and alleys, where there would be no witnesses to what he did. He would call them names and accuse them of committing crimes, just to provoke them into saying something back or hitting him or running away. If they ran away he would shoot them. If they did anything else, he would beat them up with his club and take them to the police station and charge them with resisting arrest and assaulting an officer. You couldn't win with a bully like Officer Lafferty. Louretta found herself running into the alley, her thick brown braids flying behind her, forgetting all about what Momma would think.

"Run!" she cried to the boys. "The Man is coming. Hurry!"

Ulysses and Jethro and David and Frank and the new boy who was with them didn't need to be warned twice. They knew who The Man was; someone in uniform, someone so big and brutal and powerful that he didn't need a name.

Fortunately the alley went clear through from Thirteenth Street, where Louretta had been, to the Avenue, and by the time Officer Lafferty entered the alley they had already emerged, breathless and panting, on the Avenue. Here was safety: stores and bars and restaurants and bright lights and crowds of people. Officer Lafferty would not dare bother them there. They slowed down and tried to act as if they had been strolling along the Avenue all afternoon. But they were still breathing heavily.

"Whew," Frank said. "That was close. Thanks, girl."

Louretta warmed with pride. She had done the boys a favor; maybe now they would accept her as a friend instead of teasing her about her hair. But what Frank said didn't really count. He was as light as Louretta, with a complexion like coffee with cream. It was what the others said that mattered.

"Yeah," Ulysses echoed. "My head still aches from the last time Lafferty played Chopsticks on it. It wasn't looking forward to being a drum for him again."

Louretta laughed out loud. Big, round-faced, ebony

Ulysses, rubbing his head and comparing it to a drum, was comical. He weighed almost 200 pounds and was already on the junior varsity football team at school, though he was barely fifteen. He would make the senior varsity, too, if he went out for practice after school. But he preferred hanging around with the other boys in the neighborhood. They all belonged to a gang, the Hawks, and spent most of their time planning fights with their rival gang, the Avengers.

"We need a place to hang out," David said. "The alley's no good any more. The cold weather's coming on, and the cops keep chasing us."

"Aw," Jethro said, his small chin jutting out angrily, "you guys are too scary. There's five of us and only one of him. We could have licked him easy."

"A *cop?*" David said, his eyes large and incredulous. David was the youngest of the boys, thirteen, but he was already almost six feet tall, with long arms and legs that did not go with his baby face. The boys called him "Hoss" because he looked and moved like an awkward colt. "Man, you're crazy to even think about beating up a cop. *Nobody* wins against a cop."

But Jethro, for all his small stature, still looked as if he wanted to take on the whole police force.

"Best thing to do with cops is run the other way when you see them coming," Frank said.

Louretta understood this. All the people in Southside were united in their distrust and fear of policemen. An outsider might think this meant all of them must be criminals. But this was not true. Most of the Southside people were respectable, though a few of them might have little things

8

they wanted to hide. Maybe they were on Welfare and somebody in the family was also working one or two days a week—not earning enough to live on, but enough to lose the important Welfare money if it was found out. Or maybe they played the number every day, or sold home-made wine to friends without a liquor license. Nobody in Southside thought these things were wrong, but the cops thought differently. Then, too, practically everybody in Southside had had bad experiences with mean policemen like Officer Lafferty, who liked to kick in the doors of Southside houses and beat people up. Maybe the wide-spread Southside attitude of running from policemen and never cooperating with them helped to make them mean. But Louretta didn't think so. She thought people like Officer Lafferty were just *born* mean.

Then the new boy said something startling, and every-one quieted down respectfully when he spoke.

"I think Jethro's right," he said. "As long as we run from them they'll go on beating us. We've been running too long. We've been running from The Man for three hun-dred years, and he's still chasing us. We have to stand up to him and stand our ground and maybe remove a few of his teeth to make him respect us."

Louretta stared at the new boy, shocked both by what he'd said and the way he'd said it. His speech was clear and perfect, not mumbled and drawled like most Southside speech. (It was the south side of town, but it was also called Southside because most of the people who lived there had come from the South.) He was an odd-looking person, too: short and squat, resembling a frog or an owl, with a round head and serious round eyes behind thick round tortoise-shell frames, and he was the only one of the boys who wore a tie.

"What's your name?" she asked.

"Phil Satterthwaite," he said, and stuck out his hand and smiled, adding a half-circle of flashing teeth to the other circles that composed his face. "What's yours, little girl?"

Little girl. She didn't like that. Before she took his hand and shook it she remembered Miss Hodges saying that the girl was always supposed to offer her hand first. This smart-aleck who expressed himself so confidently didn't know *everything*, after all.

"Louretta Hawkins," she said, and added self-consciously, "*Miss* Louretta Hawkins."

"Aw, don't be so fancy, you two," Ulysses said. "Fess, call her Lou. Lou, this is Fess. We call him Fess because he's smart enough to be a professor."

Frank said, "Yeah, Fess is so heavy upstairs he don't even go to Southern High with the rest of us. He goes to Emerson."

Reluctantly, Louretta felt her respect for this strange boy increasing. You had to have at least a straight B-plus average to go to Emerson High; only the top two per cent of students in the city could qualify. Her C's in math and science had kept her out.

They were all chiming in with praise for the new boy.

"Fess comes from Boston, where they speak proper English," David said.

"Yeah, and he writes poetry," Frank said. "We're going to try to get him to write us some songs."

"Cut it out, you guys," Fess said. "She'll think I'm a toasty." He winked, squinting up one of his owl-eyes.

"Course maybe she'd like that. She looks like a toasty herself."

Toasties were people who put on airs and thought they were better than everybody else. When you were light-skinned, like Louretta, darker people were always accusing you of being a toasty because that was what they expected you to be. The same thing was true if you and your family had more money or a better education or spoke better English than other people. You had to go around constantly proving that you weren't stuck-up, and just when you thought you'd proved it once and for all, someone else would become suspicious.

Louretta felt herself getting very angry at this new boy. She'd known him less than a minute, and he'd already managed to insult her twice.

"He ain't no toasty," David said. "He whipped LeRoy Smith the first week he moved on the block."

Louretta was impressed. LeRoy Smith, boss of the Avengers, was a big boy, rough and tough for his age, who had most of the younger boys terrified. She didn't like fighting—there was too much of it in the neighborhood—but she understood the reason for it when there were bullies like LeRoy around. This new boy must be very good with his hands, and that was why the others looked up to him. They wouldn't respect him for his brains. No, they would admire his fighting ability, and tolerate his intelligence because of it. Frank had always been the leader of the Hawks, but now that this new boy had licked the rival gang leader, he might be taking over. The others certainly seemed to be deferring to him.

"Aw, she's no toasty either," Jethro said. "Louretta's real regular."

Louretta looked at Jethro gratefully. His small, sharp-featured face was merry.

"Even," he added, "if she does have red hair."

"Jethro Jackson! You devil!" she screeched. "I do *not* have red hair!"

But he was already streaking up the Avenue, darting nimbly in and out of crowds, stopping now and then to turn a laughing face that mocked her. She chased him, screaming, past the groceries with their baskets of fruits and vegetables on the sidewalk, past two noisy bars, past the dry cleaners and the drug store and the Jazz Joint with its recorded music blaring out on the sidewalk, past the rummage-sale stores and the cancellation-shoe stores and the occult shop selling magic herbs and oils and powders, until she ran smack into a large, soft bosom that knocked what wind she had left out of her.

When she looked up and saw it was Reverend Mamie Lobell, she was so embarrassed she wanted to die. Reverend Mamie Lobell was a tall, heavy, dignified woman who had her own church, the Cheerful Baptist Church, right here on the Avenue. She was one of Momma's best friends, though Momma did not go to her church because *she* was a Methodist, and she was a very stern and religious and forbidding person. What would Momma say when Miss Mamie told her she had seen her daughter running and screeching like a banshee, chasing a boy on the Avenue, and that Louretta had bumped right into her?

Louretta tried to smooth her hair and gather up her

spilled books and apologize all at once. "I'm sorry, Miss Mamie. I didn't see you. I wasn't looking where I was going."

But Miss Mamie was not angry; she had other things on her mind. "That's all right, child. You didn't hurt me. Look out of the way, though, the men are coming out with the furniture. Watch out there," she called in her big booming voice. "Be careful with that crucifix."

Louretta stared as a moving man came out of the church with six folding chairs, three over each arm, and a carved cross held in front of him, like a figure in a religious procession. The building was exactly like the stores on either side of it, except that its big glass window had green curtains that were always closed, and the name of the church painted on it in gold letters, with "M. Lobell, Pastor" underneath. The church had been here as long as Louretta could remember. No one in Southside thought it strange for a church to be in a store-front building between a tobacco store and an occult store, pouring out religious music and hand-clapping to mingle with the jazz and jukebox sounds of the Avenue. There were churches like the Cheerful Baptist Church in every block.

Louretta had never been inside the church, but she had often wanted to go there, because the music sounded better than the music at the Methodist Tabernacle. Often she had passed by and heard tambourines, and drums, and a piano played with a lively, bouncing rhythm that made her feet want to dance. Now, for the first time in her memory, the curtains were open. She looked inside. The large room was bare except for the religious pictures on the walls and an old dark upright piano and the purple-draped altar which the men were about to move. Most of the things were already loaded on the van at the curb.

"Are you moving the church, Miss Mamie?"

"Yes, child. It's taken us many years, but the Lord has finally found us a bigger and better home."

The man, after carrying the altar to the truck, closed the door of the building and padlocked it.

"Miss Mamie, they forgot the piano!" Louretta said excitedly.

"Oh, we're leaving it behind, Louretta. That piano is so old it might fall apart if we tried to move it. We have a new piano at our new church. Sixteenth and Pearl Streets. I want you to come to the dedication services this Sunday, and bring your mother, too."

Louretta promised, though she knew Momma wouldn't go to any church but her own, and turned back to the window, barely saying good-by to Miss Mamie. She was too excited about the piano. She pressed her nose to the glass, between the "R" and the "C" of "Church." A piano that nobody wanted! Just sitting there waiting for anybody who wanted to use it! Louretta had had six months of lessons, but never a piano of her own. She would give anything to have a piano, to practice classical pieces, and play popular songs by ear, and accompany herself while she sang. At the Methodist church she only played stately chords for hymns, but maybe in time she could learn to make the piano dance and bounce and ripple, the way the Baptist pianist had done. She felt that *that* piano would almost know how to play good music all by itself. All she would need to do would be to place her hands on the keys. The high, awkward shape of the piano was barely visible in the gathering

14

darkness, but she continued to stare, until the boys caught up and crowded around her.

"Hey!" Jethro said, the chase forgotten. "What you cats doin'? You plannin' to go to church tonight and get your souls saved?"

"The church has split, man," Ulysses said. "The joint is empty."

"This would be a good place to hang out this winter," David said wistfully.

"A *church?*" Jethro said scornfully. "You couldn't get me into a church!"

"It's not a church anymore," Fess said. "It's just a building."

"There's even a piano," Louretta said. "You fellows could sing all you wanted, and I could play for you."

"No. You'd play church chords," Jethro said with disdain. "Girls like you always play church chords. That's probably all that piano knows how to play anyway. Church chords."

"What's wrong with church chords?" Fess wanted to know.

Louretta was confused; now the new boy was coming to her rescue.

"You squares down this way," he went on, "think everything has to sound like it came from outer space, or it isn't music. But hip folks know the new sound is called 'soul,' and it comes straight from the church."

Jethro said, "Gee, I'd like to dig me some of those soul sounds, man."

"You should go to church, then," Louretta said primly, glad she had found a way to get back at Jethro.

Her triumph was cut short by the sounds of a hammer on the door beside them. It didn't take long. The man who was hammering finished and got back into his car, and they read the sign:

RENT
Four Rooms & Store
Weinstein
RA 3-6200

Their spirits fell, and their excitement vanished instantly.

"Well, there goes our hangout," Ulysses said glumly. "Where would we get the money to rent it?"

"It was a beautiful idea, man," David said.

"Oh, you cats don't do anything but talk, talk, talk and dream, dream, dream," Jethro said impatiently. "Never any action."

The new boy's owlish face was very serious. "If we want this place for a hangout," he said, "we should just *take* it. Why should we pay rent to that man? He owes it to *us*. He's probably gotten rich off our people already."

"I'm with you," Jethro said. "Maybe we can break in the back way. I'll go see." And quick as a flash, he disappeared up the alley.

Louretta was disturbed both by what Fess had said and by the way Jethro had reacted to it. Southside boys, especially restless ones like Jethro, were always looking for action, and any excuse was a good one for having an adventure, even if it meant breaking the law. It seemed that Fess was giving the boys reasons to break the law, not just in little ways, like playing the numbers, but in big and dangerous ways.

"Maybe we can find a way to pay the rent," she said to Fess, who was still scowling seriously. "I don't think we should do it any other way."

"That's because you haven't seen the light, Little Sister," Fess said. "You need to be indoctrinated. I'm going to have to have a talk with you."

She turned away, offended by his superior attitude. She had no wish to have a talk with Fess. She knew that no amount of talking, by him or by anyone else, could convince her that she had a right to take something that belonged to someone else.

Jethro, back from his expedition, sounded regretful. "There are two windows back there, but they have bars on them. Guess we can't break in."

The boys were disappointed. But Louretta, hurrying home because it was dark now and she was late for supper, was relieved.

TWO

LOURETTA TOOK A DEEP BREATH BEFORE OPENING THE DOOR
of the little house where she lived. There was lots of love
in her family, as well as plenty of excitement and quarrels
and trouble. Life at 1308 Carlisle Street was like a circus,
with something always going on in at least three places at
once. You never had time to think about yourself; you just
tried to deal with each emergency as it came up—a fight between the twins, a bone stuck in little Randolph's throat,
the baby crying—and go on to the next one. It was fun, like
any circus, but going to the circus once a year was one
thing, Louretta thought; living with it all the time was something else.

Besides Momma, there were eight Hawkinses in the
little five-room house: William, who was twenty-one; Arneatha, who was seventeen; Louretta, fourteen; Andrew
and Gordon, twelve and ten; the twins, Clarice and Bernice,
seven; and little Randolph, who was going on four. And
now Cora Lee made nine.

The house had a living room and kitchen downstairs
and three bedrooms upstairs. Louretta shared the double
bed in her room with Clarice and Bernice, who were get-

ting bigger and taking up more room all the time. They constantly poked her with their sharp knees and elbows, but she slept between them anyway to keep them from fighting with each other, which would *really* keep her awake. Momma and Arneatha and the baby and Randolph had big beds and two little cribs in the big front bedroom, and the three boys slept in the third room.

Of course William was not a boy any longer; he was a man, and ever since Poppa had gone away four years ago, he was *the* man of the house. Louretta did not like to remember that time, because Momma and Poppa had argued with each other every night. It just seemed that one day Poppa had been sitting at the head of the table, and the next day, William was there in his place. Not long after that, Randolph was born. And ever since, William seemed to be doing everything he could to take Poppa's place. He was almost as good as a real father, because he was everything a big brother should be: tall, strong, handsome, kind, stern enough to make you obey him, but pleasant enough to have fun with. Louretta didn't know what Momma would do without William. She didn't know what *any* of them would do without him. He had finished high school, and he had a good job at the post office, supervising the men who sorted the mail. Arneatha worked, too, as a housekeeper for several families, but she went to work only when she felt like it, and she spent most of her money on clothes. So it was William who really supported the family.

Besides his job at the post office, William had a secret ambition: He wanted to be a printer.

But whenever he mentioned this, Momma would get angry and say, "Don't be talking to me about buying no printing press, boy. Where would I put a printing press in this house? And if you quit your job, how would I feed this family?"

It did no good for William to explain to Momma that he would not give up his job, at least not at first; that he would do his printing in the evenings, the same way he had gone to school to learn about it. Momma simply would not listen. Louretta understood how she felt—she was scared of losing William's pay check—but she sympathized with William. She hated to take sides in arguments between Momma and William, though.

They reminded her of the old fights between Momma and Poppa, long ago. Now as then, she loved them both and wanted them both to win.

There was another thing about William that worried Momma even more; he wanted to marry Shirley Turnbo, who was a schoolteacher and a very nice lady. Every time William brought Shirley around the house, Momma was polite to her. Too polite, as if she didn't really like Shirley, but didn't dare to admit it. Louretta always tried to be extra nice to Shirley to make up for Momma's coldness, but it didn't help, and pretty soon William stopped bringing Shirley home. That made Momma feel better, but Louretta knew William still went to Shirley's house all the time.

Louretta was not as sympathetic about this problem of William's as she was about the printing press. She didn't ever want to get married—oh, maybe sometime, when she was very old, twenty-five or thirty, but not for a long time —and she didn't understand why anybody else would want to. When she grew up she wanted to have a place all her very own, at least for a while. Marriage meant a whole house full of babies to feed and take care of, and noise and yelling and fights, and no place to sit down, and no place to have your friends in and no place to even hear yourself think.

That was how it was, as usual, in the kitchen when Louretta walked in. Gordon and Andrew were in their places but playing at fighting, hitting each other with little rabbit punches, and the twins were chasing each other around the table, and Randolph was yelling while William held him on his lap and painted iodine on his skinned knee. Momma, at the stove dipping up plates of beans and greens, looked as if tears to match Randolph's might soon start trickling down her face.

Only Arneatha, sitting next to Momma's place and painting her long oval nails with Silver Frost, looked calm. She was always calm, as if she were not really a part of this family and nothing that happened in it could ever touch her. Louretta disliked Arneatha's attitude, because it was selfish, but she envied it sometimes.

Louretta slid into the chair next to her big sister. Sometimes, if she was in a good mood, Arneatha would let Louretta use her nail polish.

"Can I have some when you're finished?"

Arneatha was not in a good mood. "No," she said without looking up, and lowered her head until the long black eyelashes touched her cheeks. She held out her hand and fanned out her fingers to admire them. "Silver Frost is too grown up for you."

"Arneatha," Momma said, "I hear that baby crying. Can you go up and get her and give her her bottle?"

"I can't go now, Momma, my fingernails are wet."

"*You* go, Louretta," Momma ordered. "And when you come back, I want to know where you've been all this time."

Oh-oh. Louretta thought she had sneaked into the kitchen without being noticed.

"Yes, ma'am," she said, and went upstairs to answer the baby's thin, piercing wails. Cora Lee was dry, and when she picked her up, she instantly stopped crying. She was used to her Aunt Louretta, and knew her better than her own mother. When either Momma or Louretta picked Cora Lee up, she stopped crying, but when Arneatha took the baby, she cried even louder.

Cora Lee was nine months old now, and getting too heavy for Louretta to carry. She had to take her time bringing her downstairs, carefully planting both feet on each step before she reached her toe down to the next one. She was in no great hurry anyway. Momma was waiting to question her about where she had spent the afternoon, and she would have to tell the truth. There was something in Momma's steady, all-seeing eyes that made it impossible to lie to her. Momma always said the Lord would punish liars, and since her mother went to church so much, Louretta believed the Lord would do whatever she said. So she never lied to her, even at times, like now, when the truth was something Momma would not like to hear.

But Momma had forgotten about Louretta's lateness. When Louretta came back she was deep in a conversation with William. Louretta shifted the baby to her left arm, opened the refrigerator, got the bottle and held it under the hot water tap to warm it. Arneatha made no move to help her, though Cora Lee was much too heavy for Louretta to hold in two arms, let alone one. When she finally sat down and settled Cora Lee on her lap and gave her the bottle, her left arm felt as if it had been pulled out of its socket. But she said nothing to her older sister, only gave her a sidewise glance and saw her sitting there, her beautiful profile tilted up, looking at nothing except her drying nails.

"I put thirty dollars down on a printing press today, Momma," William said, after putting Randolph in his high chair and telling Andrew and Gordon to be quiet and making the twins sit down by smacking one of them on the rear. (You never knew which twin had done what or which one you were smacking; you just whacked the nearest one, and it had a quieting effect on both.)

"Well, you can just go get your thirty dollars back," Momma said. "I told you and told you, there's no room for any of your machinery in here."

"I don't have to keep it here, Momma," William said. He had evidently given this a great deal of thought. "Freddy James is going to let me keep it in his garage until I find a cheap place for rent."

"I don't like that Fred James, I never did," Momma said. "Before he got that car repairing business, he was in jail. Did he put you up to this? Or was it that fancy school-teacher friend of yours? I bet it was her. She's a toasty. She's not content to have a boy friend with a good job. No, she wants a *businessman*."

It was no use pointing out to Momma that practically every young man in the neighborhood except William had been in jail. Policemen like Officer Lafferty constantly arrested Southside fellows whether they had done anything wrong or not. Often whole groups of them were picked up "on suspicion" just for standing on a corner. Weeks would go by before they saw a judge and were released, and by that time they had records.

"Leave Shirley out of this, Momma," William said. His voice was even, but his lower lip was beginning to tremble, a sign to Louretta that he was upset. "She's not a toasty. She's real regular, and if you tried to be half as nice to her as she is to you, you'd see that. Besides, you ought to know by now that owning a printing press is my own idea. I've wanted one ever since high school." He was really upset; he lit a cigarette in the middle of the meal, which was something William never did, because Momma disapproved of smoking at the table. As if this gave her permission, Arneatha reached out for William's pack and lit one too.

"Raise children to be decent and they grow up and sit at the table and smoke like chimneys," was Momma's comment about this.

"Momma," William said, waving his cigarette excitedly, "I wish you'd try to see it my way just once. I went to night school for two years to become a printer. If I don't get the press soon I'll forget everything I learned. I don't want to let all that training go to waste."

"Well, I never wanted you to go to night school in the first place. You had a good job already. What did you need to go to school for?"

That was the essence of Momma's philosophy, Louretta thought: Be safe, hold on to what you have, don't reach out for anything bigger or better, or the world, the white world, will punish you. Stay in your place, even if it's a miserable corner, and hang on to what you have. Something must have frightened Momma terribly when

24

she was growing up down South to make her so scared, Louretta thought.

"Besides, if you want to be a printer why do you have to have your own printing press? Why can't you work for somebody else?"

"You know the answer, Momma. You have to be in the union to work in someone else's shop. They won't let colored guys join the union."

This was why Louretta had heard William tell Gordon and Andrew that they had to go to college. If they wanted to work at trades—as carpenters or plumbers or electricians—they would not be allowed to join the white unions. Girls didn't have to go to college—they could always be clerks or secretaries—but a boy, if he was colored, had either to be a janitor or a college graduate. There was nothing in between. Momma always said, "Well, be janitors, then. I'll never have the money to send you to college." But Louretta knew that was one reason why William wanted the printing press, to make extra money to send Gordon and Andrew and Randolph to school.

Momma looked as if she was about to cry. "I don't know why you children can't be content with the good things you've got, instead of always trying to get into something else where you're not wanted. If you give up that job at the post office, William, how will we live?"

"On Welfare," he said angrily. "With nine kids they'd give you more money than I make anyway."

Louretta knew this hurt Momma. The one thing she was proud of was that they had never had to go on Welfare.

Momma looked up to Heaven, and one tear did start

down her face. "Oh, Lord," she cried, "how much more trouble are You going to send me?"

William was up in an instant, putting his arms around Momma. "Look, we won't talk about it any more. We'll live, Momma, don't worry. I promise you I won't quit my job."

Momma sobbed louder, but she dried her tears with the corner of her apron. Soon her crying would be over, and she would go about the house again, doing her work with dry eyes and a set expression, talking only to the Lord because these children didn't understand her. It was a good time to change the subject.

"Momma," Louretta said, "the baby won't eat any more. She isn't hungry."

"Give her to me, then," Momma said, and held out her strong brown arms that seemed made for holding babies.

"Why don't you make Arneatha take her?" Louretta cried. She hadn't meant to say that, but it grieved her terribly that Arneatha, who did nothing to help the family, always got her way about everything, while William, dear good William, who worked so hard for them, couldn't get Momma to understand him even a little bit.

"Arneatha's going out in a little while," Momma said calmly, and took the baby.

"Well, why don't you make her stay home?" Louretta said. It wasn't fair that Arneatha could spend fifty dollars on a cinnamon-colored wig, which made her look silly and didn't help anybody, while William could not get a printing press to help him make more money for the family.

26

It never occurred to Momma to give William credit because he was so hard-working and ambitious instead of being a bum or a jailbird like most of the Southside fellows his age. If anything, Momma gave herself the credit because she had nursed him for five years while he was recovering from polio, which kept him in the house so that he couldn't get out to join a gang and run wild and get into trouble like all the other boys. William himself often said polio was the best thing that ever happened to him. When he finally got well, he had lost the opportunity to make friends his age, so he devoted all his time to making up the schoolwork he had missed instead. He still limped a little, but you hardly noticed it, and now he had a good job and a high school diploma and the printing diploma too, while the other Southside fellows his age had nothing but prison records. And once you had a jail record—even if it was only for "suspicion"—there was nothing to do but get into more trouble, because no one would hire you. Louretta believed her big brother could do anything he wanted, including running a successful printing business. She didn't understand why Momma didn't have the same confidence in him.

She was so lost in her thoughts she barely heard Momma saying, "You leave Arneatha alone and eat your dinner."

Louretta stared down at her cold plate. This was one of the meatless nights; no matter how carefully they stretched William's pay check, they couldn't make it buy meat for all of them more than once a week, plus fish on Saturdays and chicken on Sundays. Louretta didn't mind having beans and greens for supper because Momma flavored them with cured neck bones that gave them a delicious meaty taste. She thought they were lucky to have meat once a week; most of the Southside kids, especially the ones on Welfare, never had meat at all, except the nasty, cardboard-tasting canned meat they gave away at the Surplus Food Center. But she didn't like having her dinner cold, just because that lazy Arneatha was too busy painting her fingernails to take care of her own baby. It wasn't fair, Louretta thought. There were a lot of things in this family that weren't fair.

She could hardly wait until Momma took Cora Lee out of the room to speak to William. Fortunately Arneatha left too, to finish dressing for her date, and the other kids scampered into the living room to watch their favorite Western on TV. Only Louretta and William were left at the table. It was a rare moment in this house, a chance to have a private conversation.

She looked over at her big brother. His face had a faraway look, as if he wanted to be somewhere else. It suddenly seemed to Louretta that Momma was making a terrible mistake to be so scared of losing William. If she went on trying to control him, she was likely to cause the very thing she feared, and drive him away. The way to keep William was to let him do whatever he wanted. Otherwise, one day he would just get up and leave, like Poppa. And then what would they do? Louretta was frightened by the sadness in William's face. To cheer him up she said, "How's the mill, Brother Bill?"

This was a little rhyming game they had played together ever since Louretta was a tiny girl, something they had between them that no one else in the family shared.

The "mill" was the place where William worked, which was kind of silly, but it always got even sillier as they went along.

William smiled, and his big homely-handsome face broke into a grin that created a hundred wrinkles in his cheeks and forehead and around his eyes, like the gay ripples made by a stone tossed into the water.

"Makes me blue, Sister Lou," he replied with a chuckle.

"Take a pill, Brother Bill," she answered instantly.

He laughed. "That won't do, Sister Lou."

"Yes it will, Brother Bill."

"Can't top you, Sister Lou," he said. "You're too sharp for me tonight. I always said you had all the brains in the family. Wish I could be as smart as you."

"You never will, Brother Bill," she teased. They both laughed. Then she became serious. "Listen, William, I'll show you just how smart I am. I know a place where you can keep your printing press."

"Where?" he asked intently. Then his face fell back into sadness, the jolly wrinkles disappearing one by one. "Ah, what's the use, Lou?" he sighed, and lit a cigarette. "Momma will never go along with it. You heard what she said."

Louretta became impatient. Sometimes she thought those years at home recovering from polio, when William depended on Momma for everything, had made him her little boy for life. William was a man with everyone else, but he would always be a little boy with Momma. He would never do anything without asking her permission.

"Oh, William!" she said, and banged on the table. "You're a man now. You're not supposed to go on asking

Momma's permission for everything. You're supposed to go ahead and do what you want, and let her get used to it."

William looked thoughtful. "Maybe you're right, Lou. It *is* time I stopped letting Momma hold me back with her old-fashioned ideas."

"She thinks she's still down South on a farm," Louretta said. "She doesn't realize we're up North in a big city, and things are different now."

"You're right," he said. "I think she still thinks this is Mississippi, where we're supposed to labor in the cotton fields, and somebody will lynch me if I dare to go in business for myself. You can't tell her it's not like that up here."

"You know how Momma is," Louretta said. "She's old-fashioned, but she'll get used to the printing press once you get it. I promise you she will. And I know the perfect place for your printing shop, William. I'll tell you all about it on one condition."

William laughed. "No, no. No conditions, Lou. I'm not going to let the women in this family run me any more, remember? What's the use of getting out from under Momma's thumb if I start taking orders from you?"

He was teasing her. Louretta was embarrassed. "Oh, William, *please*," she said. "I'm not trying to give you orders. There's much more space in this building than you need for your business. If you would just let the kids have one room for a clubhouse—"

"What kids? What kind of clubhouse?" he asked suspiciously.

"Oh, the kids my age. *You* know. We need a place where we can sing, and play the piano, and play records, and dance. And there's a piano already there, William. It doesn't belong to anybody. We could use it all we wanted—"

He interrupted her. "If you mean Jethro Jackson and that gang of hoodlums, I don't want you hanging around with them. They might get you into trouble."

Louretta didn't know what to say. Of course Jethro and his friends were hoodlums, if being a hoodlum meant belonging to a gang and fighting a lot and occasionally stealing things just for adventure, but there just weren't any other kids for Louretta to be friends with. Besides, if they had a place of their own, maybe they wouldn't be hoodlums any more. William *had* to go along with her plan.

"How can they get into trouble?" she argued. "You'll be there every night. They won't dare do anything wrong with you around to keep an eye on them."

William shook his head. "I expect to be busy with my printing business. I don't want to spend my evenings being a baby sitter."

"We're not babies!" Louretta cried angrily. William was her favorite brother, and she was his favorite sister, but he did have a habit of teasing her too much. It was so hard to have grown-up thoughts, and still be only fourteen, and have older brothers and sisters who kept treating you like a child. Next he would be calling her Red.

"I'm sorry, Red. I know you and your friends are men and women. Or you think you are."

Louretta could never get angry with William. She always got hurt instead. She felt her face screw up as if she were going to cry.

William must have seen it, because he said, in a softer

voice, "Okay, Lou. Forget what I said, huh? I know how sensitive you are about your hair. Forgive me. Where is this place?"

"You know Reverend Mamie Lobell's church?"

He nodded. "That's a good-sized building. And it's right around the corner. But they have church there every night."

"Not any more. The church has moved. The place is empty now, and it's for rent. All you have to do is call up this number." She handed him the piece of paper on which she had written the name, Weinstein, and the phone number.

"Probably can't afford it anyway." William shrugged, and got up, and put on his jacket to go out to the phone booth on the corner. "Oh, well, no harm in trying. Here, Lou." From inside his jacket he withdrew a thin envelope and handed it to her. "While I'm gone you can try out this new record."

She opened it eagerly. It was the latest number by the Dacrons, "If You Knew What I Know," with a fast number on the other side. She ran into the front room, put it on the little portable record player, and turned off the television set. The children yelled in protest until they heard the new music. Then nobody minded. They would rather dance, the whole family of them, to a new record than do anything else, even watch TV, and all of them could dance very well.

First Andrew danced with Gordon, and Bernice with Clarice, then Andrew started dancing with one of the twins, and Gordon with the other, while Louretta danced all by herself. Even Momma, tired as she was after a day of housework and worried as she was about William, got out in the middle of the floor and danced, holding Cora Lee on her shoulder. Momma was the best dancer of them all; she had a way of shuffling in her slippers so that her feet barely seemed to move, but really, when you looked, you saw that every part of her body was in gentle motion. The baby loved Momma's dancing and gurgled with pleasure over her shoulder.

Wanting to prolong the fun, Louretta put a whole stack of old records on the machine. At that moment Arneatha's boy friend John Hoxter arrived and began dancing with Arneatha, swinging and spinning her so wildly that her wig went crooked and fell over one eye. Louretta laughed and laughed at this. She took her baby brother's hands and joined him in the little jig Randolph called "dancing," taking little baby steps to match his.

Then William came back from making his phone call. Limping just a little, he crossed the room, put his arm around Louretta's waist, and started to cut a rug with her. It was the fast side of the new record, but William could keep up with it; he didn't let his limp stop him from anything. Except for Momma, he was the best dancer in the family.

"How much do they want for it?" she whispered as she danced past him.

"Only twenty-five a month," he said out of the side of his mouth.

"Are you going to take it?"

Instead of answering, he spun her around, let go of her, clapped his hands, and said, "Boogaloo, Sister Lou."

Laughing, she obeyed, swaying her hips and snapping her fingers.

The entire family was dancing now, Arneatha with John Hoxter, Gordon with Clarice, Andrew with Bernice, and Momma with Cora Lee on her shoulder. In the corner little Randolph, happy because he had not yet been put to bed, skipped merrily to a dance of his own. The floor of the little house shook with the stamping of their feet, and the ceiling rang with their laughter. They didn't have much room or much money, and they had only had beans for supper, but sometimes, Louretta thought, they had more fun than any other family in town.

THREE

LOURETTA CAME RUSHING OUT OF THIRD PERIOD ENGLISH
class with a happy buzzing in her head. Miss Hodges, the
pretty little brownskinned teacher, had praised Louretta to
the rest of the class. Most of them had not even done their
homework, which was to read three poems by Longfellow,
but Louretta had not only done the reading, she had mem-
orized one poem all the way through—without even trying!

First Miss Hodges had asked Joella Evans what she
thought Longfellow had meant when he wrote "A Psalm of
Life."

Joella had stumbled, and said, "He mean—he mean—I
don't know *what* he mean, ma'am. It don't make much
sense to me."

"It *doesn't* make much sense, you mean," Miss Hodges
had said. "How can it make sense if you didn't read it?
Admit it, Joella, you didn't do your homework. . . . Louretta?"

"I think Longfellow means we should take life seriously, and not waste our time, and try to get our work
done," Louretta had said.

"Very good, Louretta. Can you tell us which lines in the poem say that to you? Can you recite them?"

Louretta had liked the poem because the words seemed to sing, as if they should be set to music, and she had read it to herself aloud several times the night before. When she stood she found the words singing in her head, and though at first her voice faltered, at the end she was reciting in a clear, ringing voice—

> Let us, then, be up and doing,
> With a heart for every fate;
> Still achieving, still pursuing,
> Learn to labor and to wait.

There had been a stunned silence when she finished, and then Louretta had added, "The message isn't just in a few lines, it's in the whole poem, Miss Hodges. I guess that's why I recited the whole thing."

"Wonderful, Louretta. You not only learned the poem, you took its message to heart. I wish the *rest* of this class could learn to be as conscientious as Longfellow wants us to be."

Louretta hadn't known what *conscientious* meant, but she understood that Miss Hodges was very, very pleased with her, and for the rest of the hour, she had sat there in a warm, pleasant haze, her head buzzing with excitement, scarcely paying attention. Now the bell had rung, and she was still in a glow. Looking around for someone to share her happiness with, she spied Donna DeMarco talking to a couple of boys.

Donna had been Louretta's best friend when they were little girls. The DeMarco family had lived on Carlisle

Street then, three doors away from the Hawkinses, because the neighborhood was still what was called "mixed," and life then had been very mixed and jolly indeed, with the little girls eating spaghetti at Donna's house one day and beans at Louretta's the next, and playing together all the time.

But when they were both about nine, the DeMarco family had moved away, like all the other Italian and Polish and Jewish families, and Louretta had not seen Donna again until high school. They were still friends, but something was different, and when school was over they no longer went to each other's houses—they went separate ways. Louretta didn't know what had changed, exactly, but she knew it had something to do with boys. All the white girls at school had a way of becoming suddenly unfriendly when white boys were around.

Normally, seeing Donna talking to a pair of boys, she would have passed her by in the hall, but today she was so excited that she failed to heed the warning. She walked right up to Donna and said, "Oh, Donna, wasn't it wonderful what Miss Hodges said to me about the poem?"

The boys, both big, blond football players, stopped their lively talking as soon as Louretta approached and began shifting their feet awkwardly.

"Oh," Donna said, "of course she'd say that to *you*."

"What do you mean?"

"I mean she's bound to be on your side. But *I* thought it sounded funny, if you want to know, hearing you recite that poem in your funny accent. Of course Miss Hodges wouldn't even notice it," Donna added.

"You've got a nerve, talking about *my* accent," Louretta retorted. "Your mom and pop can hardly speak English!"

Donna reddened, but fought back. "So what? They can still read poetry, and write it too, if they want. I bet you never even heard of Dante."

Louretta was silent.

"Of course not," Donna concluded with a toss of her blue-black pony tail. "*Your* people never wrote any poetry. All they did was dig the fields and pick cotton and do housework. I think *you* ought to stick to things like that too."

Louretta was too hurt and angry to say anything. There was a roaring in her head and a mist before her eyes that made her see two Donnas, both looking at her with scorn, and four boys instead of two, all grinning with amusement. She knew Donna had only acted this way because she did not want the boys to think Louretta was a friend of hers. But that did not make it any better. Numb as if she had been slapped, she walked away resolved never, never to speak to Donna again.

Joella Evans, looking sulky, came out of the classroom. Miss Hodges had detained her after class, probably to scold her for not doing her homework. Joella was a heavy-set girl with full lips, and when she was angry, as she was now, she poked out her lips even further. Louretta walked over to her. She didn't need Donna, she could have other friends.

"Listen, Joella," she said, "I'd be glad to explain that poem to you. If you want, I can help you with your homework every night. Why don't you come over to my house after school?"

There wasn't much room at home, of course, but maybe she and Joella could use the kitchen to study after everyone had finished dinner. She tried to slip her arm through Joella's. The other girl angrily pulled her arm away.

"I don't need you or nobody else to 'splain things to me," she said. "You think you're so cute because you're Miss Hodges' pet, but I saw you trying to talk to those white kids. You got a bad case of the white fever, ain't you?"

"White fever" was the disease of someone who was so eager for white friends that she would make a fool of herself in order to have them. Louretta wanted to explain that she did not have this disease, that she had simply approached Donna because they used to be friends. "No, Joella, that's not true. I just—" she began.

"It's no wonder you have the fever, looking the way you do. But it ain't nothing to be proud of," Joella said.

"What do you mean?" Louretta said angrily.

"Ask your mother," Joella taunted, and switched off down the hall, toward the boys' end, where Frank and Ulysses and Jethro waited. Louretta wanted to follow, but she hung back, afraid that they might not want her around either. They might tease her about having red hair.

Being called "Red" had always made Louretta angry, but she had never fully understood why until now. It was not merely a way of setting her apart, and making fun of what was different about her; it was also a way of saying something bad about her mother. In Louretta's neighborhood, to say something bad about someone's mother was to invite him to try to kill you. If a Southside boy wanted to start a fight, all he had to say to another boy was, "Your mother—." He didn't even have to finish the sentence. The other boy would tear into him, fists flying, in a blind fury, and would not stop fighting until he was thoroughly beaten. Louretta had always reacted with the same fury whenever someone accused her of having red hair, but she had never before known why.

Joella had joined the Southside boys. They were laughing and joking and doing little dance steps at the far end of the hall. At the other end, Donna and her boy friends were laughing too.

Louretta, hearing both groups, stood alone in the middle. Her eyes were dry, and she leaned against the wall with a nonchalance that said she didn't need anybody, but inside, she ached because she didn't seem to belong *anywhere*. Her back was firmly turned on Donna and her friends, but she felt she could not join the group at the other end, either—without doing something that would prove to them that she was not really different, no matter how she looked.

If only William would rent the building and let the kids use part of it. But when she asked him about it, all he would say was "Don't know" or "We'll see" or "Have patience, Red."

Louretta thought of the line, "Learn to labor and to wait." She didn't mind labor, but waiting was something she couldn't stand very much of.

Afraid Joella had said something to the Hawks about her, she didn't stop to talk to them today. It was early when she got home. The house was quiet, but it was full of smoke and the sharp odor of burning hair. Louretta knew what that meant.

She went to the kitchen and found Arneatha sitting with a towel around her shoulders while Momma straightened her hair with a brass comb which she heated on the stove. Momma was half finished, so one side of Arneatha's hair stuck out in a great fluffy cloud, while the other side hung as straight and shiny as silk.

"Press it hard, Momma," Arneatha said. "I want it to last till the party on Saturday."

"If I pressed it any harder you'd be bald," Momma said, and flipped the lock of hair she had finished forward, over Arneatha's face.

"Ow!" Arneatha screeched, her voice muffled by hair. "It's still steaming!"

Louretta couldn't help giggling; her sister looked so funny, with one side of her hair all puffed up and the other straight, and one lock falling over her indignant face.

"What are you laughing about, Missy?" Momma wanted to know. "You're next. Take the pins out of your hair and get out of your good clothes. And when the twins get home, you get *them* ready, too."

"Oh, *Momma*," Louretta complained. The twins hated to get their hair washed, and she hated the job of getting them ready. But when Momma decided it was hair-washing day, there was nothing to do but go along with it. She took off her blouse, pinned a towel around her neck, and removed the pins that held her heavy brown plaits on top of her head. When the plaits were undone her thick hair hung to below her shoulders and fanned out in crinkly waves on either side. She took a large hunk of it between her thumb and forefinger and pulled it forward for a good look. It was dark brown, without even a glint of red.

Nevertheless she said, "Momma, when you wash my hair, will you dye it black, like yours and Arneatha's?"

Momma stopped working on Arneatha's hair and stared at her. "Whatever for, child? Your hair's a beautiful color."

"I don't like it," Louretta said softly.

"I don't believe in dyeing hair," Momma said. "I don't even dye these gray hairs of mine, because I believe the Lord gives everybody what she's supposed to have—hair, eyes, skin and all—and they all go together. Louretta, black hair would be ugly on you."

"Lord knows she's ugly enough as it is," Arneatha murmured.

"I suppose you think *you're* Lena Horne," Louretta shot back at her sister—then regretted it, because Arneatha's pretty profile did resemble the movie star's. Though at the moment, with her hair disarranged, she resembled a sheepdog more.

"No," Arneatha replied, "but at least I look like I belong in this family."

Momma put down the hot comb again. "Just what are you trying to say, Miss Arneatha?" she demanded.

Now Arneatha seemed embarrassed. "*You* know," she said.

Louretta knew too. She glanced down at her light tan arms. All the rest of them, from Momma right on down to Randolph, were the warm, smooth brown of milk chocolate.

Momma just stood there, her hands on her hips. "I'm waiting. Come on out and say it."

But Arneatha didn't say anything. She just looked scared.

"All right, I'll say it for you, then. You're trying to say you think Louretta had a different father from the rest of you kids. A white father. Is that what you think?"

Louretta put her hands over her ears. This was what they all meant when they teased her and called her "Red". She didn't want to hear it. But Momma's voice seeped through her fingers.

"—well, I think that's pretty funny, coming from you. At least I was married before any of my children were born. But since that's what you think of your mother, Arneatha, you can find someone else to do your hair."

Arneatha looked desperate. She had a date tonight, and here she was with one half of her hair all fluffed out and the other straight as cornsilk. But Momma did not even look at her again. She beckoned to Louretta instead.

"Come here, child. Let me start on you."

And while she combed Louretta's hair and shampooed it and rinsed it in the sink and dried it in a towel and separated it into sections for straightening, Momma brought out some points of family history Louretta had never known before. She was talking to Louretta, but what she said was also meant for Arneatha's ears.

"I always thought you took after your father's side of the family, Louretta. Matter of fact, you look exactly like him. You're lighter than he was, but then, there are lots of light-skinned people on his side of the family.

"Now some people think it's a disgrace for a per-

43

son to be light, because they think it has to mean her mother must have been a bad woman. But that just shows how ignorant they are. Sometimes it happens the other way around, the way it did in your father's family.

"Now I'll bet you didn't know there were once white slaves as well as colored slaves. A lot of people don't know that. But there were, and your father's grandfather married one of those slaves. He was a free Negro, born in the North, and she was a bond servant who'd come here from Wales, and she got *her* freedom by marrying *him*.

"So you see, Louretta, you don't have a thing to be ashamed of. You came by your color in a respectable way, and it's as good a color as anybody else's, and don't let anybody try to tell you any different. And don't let anbody tell you you don't belong in this family, either. You belong with us, all right. You're the spitting image of your father, eyes, nose and all. And he was a fine man. I wish all of my children took after him."

"If he was such a fine man how come he left us?" Arneatha wanted to know.

Louretta turned in her chair to look at Momma. She looked as if something had struck her.

When she spoke her voice was strained. "I never told any of you that story. William's the only one who knows. But you two are the next oldest, and I guess you have a right to know too."

Louretta felt good about what had gone before, but now she was worried. She didn't want to hear anything bad about her father. "Poppa didn't want to leave us, did he, Momma?" she cried.

44

To her great relief her mother said, "No, child, he didn't. You see, we were having a hard time feeding all of you in those days. Your father had lost his job, and there just didn't seem to be any other jobs around. We had no money for food or anything. So finally he went down to the Welfare Office—I didn't want him to, but he did—"

Now Louretta understood what those arguments so long ago had been all about, and why they had been so terrible. Going on Welfare was the worst thing that could happen to a family. It meant you had to live like a prisoner in your own house, and only spend money on necessary things, and never have any fun, and the Welfare visitor could come snooping around at any time to check up on you. Momma had never wanted it to happen to them, and that was why she had argued so much with Poppa.

"—and they told him a family with a father at home couldn't get on Welfare. A married woman with children could get Welfare money, all right, but only if her husband wasn't with her. So we talked it over, and I begged and pleaded with him—but there still wasn't any money. So he left." 75-135

It was a short story. Simple and short. But Louretta knew she would remember it a long, long time.

There was one thing she didn't understand, though. "But we never *did* go on Welfare, did we, Momma?"

"No. When William heard about what had happened, he got so mad he went downtown and got a job the very next day. Your father only went as far as the fourth grade in school, so work was scarce for him. But William, he had his high school diploma, so he didn't have no trouble finding a job."

"Well, after William got a job, why didn't you tell Poppa to come back?"

"I didn't know where he had gone. He never let me know," Momma said.

"Why not, Momma? Why not?"

Momma got down from her high stool and went over to the kitchen window. In the deepening twilight, her heavy, sagging figure and her face looked more tired than ever. "I guess," she said, "he was too ashamed."

There was silence in the kitchen for several minutes. Then Momma turned and pointed a finger at Louretta. She seemed angry, but not at Louretta, not at anyone in particular, unless it was the Lord. "But you've got nothing to be ashamed of. Nothing at all! Except, maybe, what happened to your sister, and thank the Lord, your father doesn't know about that. Wherever he is, he doesn't know."

Louretta picked up a mirror and looked at her freshly washed and dried hair. It was the same as always—long, thick, crinkly and dark brown, matching her eyes and brows and lashes. All her life she had heard people talking about "good hair" and "bad hair." Hers was neither, she decided; it was just *her* hair, the hair she was supposed to have. She began to plait it and found that its wiry texture helped her make firm plaits that stayed in place. "I don't want it dyed, Momma," she announced, "and I don't want it straightened either."

Arneatha spoke up with a whine. "I guess nobody's going to finish fixing *my* hair."

"No," Momma said. "Nobody is, Miss Lady. I guess you can just wear your false hair tonight. Or else stay home."

Arneatha began to whine. "I can't, Momma. I've got a date with John Hoxter. John Hoxter wants to marry me."

"Does he want Cora Lee too?" Momma asked.

"I don't think so, Momma," Arneatha said. "You know a man only wants to bring up his own babies."

"Well, you should have thought of that before you had yours," Momma said calmly.

"You mean you won't keep Cora Lee for me after I'm married?"

"That's exactly what I mean," Momma said. Her face was stern. "She's your child, not mine. She belongs with you."

"But Momma," Arneatha cried, "she doesn't even know I'm her mother!"

"Well, she's going to learn," Momma said, "starting right now. I'm going to services tonight. You stay home and look after her."

Louretta had never known Momma to be so hard on Arneatha before. Arneatha burst into tears. With her face twisted and her hair going every which way, she was really a sight. For the first time, Louretta felt sorry for her sister instead of envying her.

"Don't worry, Arneatha," she said softly, and touched her sister on the shoulder. "It'll work out all right. Cora Lee's a lovely baby. Maybe John Hoxter will want her. Or maybe Momma will change her mind."

"She would if it were you," Arneatha sobbed. "She favors you. She always did. Everybody favors you because you're so light."

It had been a day of surprises, but this was the biggest

one of all. To think that Arneatha was jealous of Louretta, when all the time it had seemed to be the other way around! But it was because of her color. Always her color. She wished people would forget about it and start noticing other things.

"Oh, no, that's not true, Arneatha," she said softly.

"It is! It is!" Arneatha cried.

Before any of them could say anything else, William burst into the kitchen. "Hi, Mom, 'Neatha," he said, and gave Momma a kiss. "Smells like a beauty parlor in here. But where are the beauties?" he teased.

Then he winked at Louretta. "How de do, Sister Lou," he said, and tossed a ring of jangling keys on the kitchen table.

"Those," he said, "are the keys to Number Thirteen Forty-Three on the Avenue. Formerly the Cheerful Baptist Church. And now the Hawkins Printing Press."

"Oh, William!" Louretta cried, and leaped toward him, flinging her arms around his waist because he was too tall for her to reach his neck. "You got it! You really got it!"

"Yes," he said, "and you've got your playhouse too."

"It's not a playhouse," she said indignantly. "It's a *clubhouse*."

But she was really too happy to care, though Momma had picked up the hot iron and seemed bent on straightening Louretta's hair, or burning her ears, or both.

FOUR

THERE WAS NOTHING MAGICAL ABOUT THE CITY'S UGLY, FA-
miliar streets, but Louretta felt like the Pied Piper as she
walked past crowded apartment buildings and dirty alleys
on a clear fall day after school. The string of teen-agers
trailing behind her had begun with only the five Hawks,
but without broadcasting any announcements, they were
joined by more in every block, until by the time they
reached the Avenue there were fifteen in the group—
mostly boys, but a sprinkling of girls, too, including Joella
Evans.

William was waiting there, jangling his keys and wearing a broad smile until he saw the group that was with
Louretta.

"Who are all these kids, Lou?" he demanded. "I'll bet
you don't even know their names."

"I do too," Louretta said. "My brother William—
my friends Sharon, Joella, Florence, Jethro, Frank, David,
Fess, and, and—" She stopped when she got to a buff-col-
ored, sullen-looking boy she had never seen before.

"Calvin," the boy supplied.

"—and Calvin," Louretta repeated. "You see?"

"I see, all right," William said. His eyes traveled somberly from Jethro's ragged sweater to Sharon's large stomach to Calvin's threatening scowl. "If this is the club, Lou, I think you'd better forget about having them meet here. I'm sorry."

"Aw, *shoot*, man," came from Ulysses.

"I *told* you he wouldn't let us," David said.

"What a square," Jethro replied.

Feet shuffled, tension mounted.

"You *promised*, William," Louretta pleaded.

William didn't seem to hear. He was too intent on the razor blade which had suddenly appeared in Calvin's hand. "You gonna try something, fella?" he asked the stranger.

"Yeah," Calvin said. Then a grin replaced the scowl on his face. It was like the sun coming out from behind a dark cloud. "I'm gonna try and scrape them letters off your window. Unless you still wanta call it a church."

All eyes turned to the window and its gold letters that still proclaimed "The Cheerful Baptist Church." The laughter started with Jethro, was joined by Ulysses' bass note, and quickly spread to the entire group.

William laughed last. The frown lines between his eyes vanished, and so did the group's tension.

"What you gonna call this place, man?" Calvin asked, still very serious. Louretta decided that the scowl was his habitual expression, and that it meant intense concentration, not menace. "You give me fifty cents, I get some gold paint over to the hardware store, and I letter it up for you real good."

William laughed again. "So you're an artist, huh?"

"Yeah, man, I'm an artist," Calvin replied, as if daring William to make something of it. "I had two years of lettering and drawing already. This year I take layout and illustration."

"Okay, artist," William said. "How about calling it 'The Cheerful Printing Press'? That way you'll only have to do one line over. And we could use some cheerfulness around here." He held out a dollar bill. "Keep the change."

Calvin held up a hand in refusal. "Naw, man. You don't have to pay me. I need the practice. Maybe you could just let me have a corner of this place to work in now and then. I got no room to draw at home."

Before William could answer this request, he was besieged by many others.

"Can we put in a pool table?"

"It don't cost nothing to rent a jukebox—"

"Can we have club meetings every night?"

"Oh, who wants meetings? I want to *dance!*"

From Louretta: "Can we call it 'The Cheerful *Clubhouse* and Printing Press'?"

"I thought up a better name," said Jethro. " 'The Hawks' Nest.' "

"Yeah," Frank approved. "That way the other gangs will know it's *our* place."

The worry lines had returned between William's eyes already. Brushing a dozen hands from his sleeves, he said "That's enough, all of you. Quit pushing me so hard. And that means you too, Lou."

Louretta felt herself developing the kind of temper that was supposed to go with red hair, even though hers was brown. "Listen here, William. If it hadn't been for me, you wouldn't even have this place."

"I know, Lou," he admitted. "I know I owe you a lot. If it weren't for you, I'd still be letting Momma talk me out of this. Maybe for the rest of my life." His smile came back as he watched Calvin scraping away at the window. "Sure, your friends can come here if they want. But let's see how it works out before you put your name out front. Will that do, Sister Lou?"

"Sure it will, Brother Bill," she replied, though privately she felt some doubts. Just let one little thing go wrong, and William might decide to put them all out. A million things might go wrong with these kids. She wanted to tell him he would have to be patient. But William wasn't used to the street kids; he had stayed home all through his teens. He didn't understand that no matter how they acted, you had to trust them, and they would be all right in the end.

"The main thing," William was saying, "is for me to get my business started. Nothing can interfere with that. 'Cause if my business doesn't pay, we can't pay the rent."

"Well, then, what are we waiting for?" cried Fess, who had been off to one side, quietly admiring the heavy iron printing press that stood on the sidewalk.

"Yeah," said Jethro. "Let's move this mustard plaster inside."

William unlocked the door, and half a dozen boys gathered around the press and attempted to lift it. While they strained and grunted, Jethro stood on the sidelines and gave orders.

"Lift the front end higher! Don't jiggle it! And don't

stumble! Watch where you're walking, you clumsy apes!"

"William, can I have a key?" Louretta asked her brother.

"Don't bother me now, Lou," he said absently. "Put it in the back room, boys. Against the back wall."

"Can I have a key?" she repeated, though she didn't want to try William's patience too far.

He paused in his supervising and gave her a look that seemed to say she had done just that. "No," he said. "I don't want anybody here unless I'm here, too. I signed the lease for this place. I'm responsible for what goes on here. Easy with that press, boys. Try not to drag it any more than you can help. Just lift it easy and move it nice and slow."

Louretta's dream of a hangout had come true, but it was already a disappointment. William cared more about his new business than he did about her.

After he and the boys and the press disappeared into the little back room, she looked around the large front room where she stood. In the daytime it seemed like a cave. Gray and empty and cold. Maybe that was why nearly everyone was in back with William instead of where she had pictured them, joyfully gathered around her at the piano.

It was still there, black and huge as ever, but in the daytime it didn't seem as beautiful as it had in the dark, when Louretta had first seen it. The wood was covered with scars, and when she walked over for a closer look she found that some of the keys were missing. All the rest were yellow and dirty. She touched one. It gave off a twanging, sour note.

Discouraged, Louretta looked around. Only the girls, Sharon and Joella and Florence, remained in the room with her. They were bored and restless.

"Let's sing," Louretta said hopefully.

"Shoot, no," Joella replied with an outward thrust of her lower lip. "I want to play me some records and dance."

"There ain't no record player in here," said Florence, a tall, skinny girl with boyish short hair and long pants.

"There ain't *nothin'* in here," said Sharon, whose pregnancy made her resemble a stout little middle-aged woman. She seemed very disgusted—whether about the condition of the building or about her own condition, Louretta could not tell.

"Let's go get us some sodas. Someplace where we can hear some music," Florence suggested.

"We can make our *own* music," Louretta said desperately.

But her first efforts produced more sour notes. She would have to memorize the places where the broken keys were so she could skip them when she played.

Sharon laughed. "You call that music? Sounds like a hungry cat cryin' on a back fence to me."

Louretta felt her temper return. Determined to show them, she launched into her recital piece, the last thing she had learned in her half-year of lessons, the first movement of Beethoven's "Moonlight Sonata." She thought she had forgotten it long ago, but it was still intact in her memory; she thought the old piano would not cooperate with her, but the sonata was mostly on the black keys, and somehow

54

those notes were all there, clear as crystal, sombre as moonlight, beautiful as poetry.

Somewhere in the middle she did strike a sour note, and Joella laughed, but it only reinforced Louretta's determination to finish. At the end she looked around expectantly at the girls. They looked nervous and uncomfortable, as if they didn't like having to react to something they didn't understand.

"Aw, child, that ain't music," Sharon finally said. "Whoever heard of dancing to something like that?"

Joella added, "If you ask me, it sounds like a doggone funeral march."

But Fess had joined them. "That's boss, Lou," he said. "It's got soul."

Much as she disliked Fess, Louretta almost leaped up to kiss him then.

But before she could, he added, "It's *white* soul, though. You won't really be saying anything on that piano till you get some *black* soul into it."

Louretta was close to tears. She didn't even know what "soul" meant, let alone the difference between "white" soul and "black" soul, and now Fess was implying that one was good and the other was bad. Taking his praise away as suddenly as he had given it, he returned to the back room. And the girls were moving fast toward the front door.

Louretta cried out brightly, "Let's go see what the boys are doing in the back room."

That was the most successful thing she'd said that day. Joella and Florence and Sharon turned in unison, the way Clarice and Bernice often did, as if they were connected by invisible wires. Apparently there was one thing all three were interested in. Boys.

What the boys were doing in the back room had nothing to do with music. They were helping William set up his press and get ready to run off his first job, a restaurant menu.

Louretta decided she would never really understand boys. Apparently, much as they liked singing, they liked working even better.

Fess was saying excitedly as he stacked sheets of paper, "This press is boss, man. I been thinking what we could do with it. We could put out a newspaper."

William looked up from the table where he was mixing inks. "What kind of paper you plan on publishing?"

"The truth," Fess replied instantly. "We can educate the whole neighborhood, show 'em the way to get out of slavery. 'Cause they're still slaves, make no mistake about it."

"Who's going to pay for all this?" William wanted to know.

'Aw, man, you got the press *already*. Don't be so selfish. Don't you want to do something for your people?"

"All I can see," William said quietly, "is that you're asking me to do something for *you*."

But the boys were too excited to hear him. "What we gone call the paper, man?" Frank wanted to know.

"*The Weekly Truth*," Fess replied instantly. He had evidently been thinking about this a long time.

"*Weekly?*" William asked in disbelief. But his voice was drowned out in the general clamor.

"What we gonna charge for the paper?"

"It's free. We're gonna give it away."

"Well, what we gonna put in the paper, man?" Jethro demanded.

"*The truth*, like I said," Fess said. "We gonna tell 'em all about the crooked merchants in this neighborhood, which stores to shop in and which to stay away from, and how to go down City Hall and make their landlords' give 'em heat, and who to vote for. Stuff like that."

"What about stories and poetry?" Louretta asked.

There were several loud groans. But Fess gave Louretta a thoughtful look. "The chick has a point. We won't be printing the kind of stories *she* means, though. No pretty little flower poems."

"How do you know what kind of poems I like?" Louretta cried. "You don't know anything about me."

Fess ignored her. "But I have a couple of tough poems I'd like to put in. Like, you know, the one about the lynching."

"Yeah, man. I like that one," Jethro said eagerly.

"And we can all write stories. Lots of stories."

"Not me," said Ulysses.

"Why not, man? Everybody has stories to tell. *Something* must have happened to you."

"Yeah, man, but I can't write."

"Just put it in your own words. Tell it like it is."

Ulysses still looked doubtful.

"Come on," Fess urged. "Remember something that happened to you. Right now."

Ulysses began slowly, but his voice quickened as he went on. "Well, there was the time the coach put me in at end and there was this big redhead guy on the other team, he name Big Red, and everybody scared of him, and when we line up he call me a name and he say, he say, 'If you try and tackle me today, you gone be sorry,' and I didn't say nothing to him then, but when he go back for a pass, I go after him, and I knock him down so hard he lose the ball, and we recover, and I still on top of him, and I got my hands on his windpipe, and I say to him, I say, 'White boy, you ever call me that again, you ain't never gone get another chance to call nobody nothin',' and he looked up at me, and his eyes were real mean, but he didn't dare open his mouth, and nobody ain't had no trouble out of him since."

Ulysses had said all of this in one breath, his arms waving wildly to illustrate what had happened. Now he took a deep breath. "That a story, man?"

"Sure that's a story," Fess said approvingly. "You go home and write it tonight."

The doubtful look had returned to Ulysses' face, but he promised to try.

"*Everybody* write a story this week," Fess commanded. "Then we'll pick the best ones to put in the paper."

William interrupted Fess's confident plans. "I haven't said you can print the paper yet. How'm I gonna get my work done with all of you cluttering up the place?"

Fess gave William a slow surprised look, as if he had forgotten all about him, and was just remembering that he was there.

Then, in a kindly voice, he said, "You'll get used to it, man."

FIVE

LOURETTA HUNG AROUND AFTER MISS HODGES' CLASS, WAITING
to speak to her until she had finished talking to five pupils.
Finally the room was empty except for Louretta and the
little teacher sitting at her desk shuffling papers.

She looked up pleasantly when Louretta came forward.
"Did you want to see me about the assignment, Louretta?"

"No, not about the assignment, Miss Hodges. But I
did want to see you."

"Well, what's on your mind, Louretta? I know you
don't have any problems with the work. So it must be
something else."

Louretta nodded, but couldn't find the right words to
say what she wanted.

"Never mind," she said, and started to leave the room,
knowing her face was turning dark red with confusion.
Being darker would have many advantages, she thought;
and one of them would be not being able to blush.

She was at the door when Miss Hodges' voice, almost
as uncertain as her own, called out, "Louretta?"

"Yes, ma'am?" Louretta said, turning.

"If you've got something to say to me, I wish you'd say it."

Louretta still hesitated.

Miss Hodges looked at her watch. "I wish I had more time to spend with you, Louretta. But I only have fifteen minutes before a friend of mine will pick me up to take me to her house for dinner."

Louretta shut her eyes, took a deep breath, and plunged in. "Well I was wondering if you would have any time after school to talk to a club of mine I've gotten started. It's not a club exactly, it's just a bunch of kids, and we don't exactly have a clubhouse, it's really my brother William's printing shop, but the kids want to put out a newspaper, and I think they could use some help with it. I thought they were going to have a music group, because there's a piano in the building, but it looks like they'd rather have a newspaper, and I don't know what to *do*—"

"Where is this clubhouse, Louretta?" Miss Hodges asked.

"Number 1343 on the Avenue."

"And when did you want me to come?"

Louretta's voice took on a ring of urgency. "As soon as you can, Miss Hodges. See, Fess is starting the newspaper, and I don't know what they're going to put in it, but maybe you could help them."

Miss Hodges tapped a pencil on her desk. "Who is Fess?"

"A real smart boy, Miss Hodges. A writer. He goes to Emerson. And he wants to put out this newspaper and call it *The Weekly Truth*. Everybody's going to write stories for it, but most of them don't know how. I thought maybe you could help with spelling and grammar, things like that."

"I must say this sounds interesting," Miss Hodges said. "A newspaper. Hmmmm. But you say *you* wanted to start a music group?"

"Oh, yes, Miss Hodges. You see, there's a piano there that the church left behind, and Jethro and Ulysses and the others always used to sing in the alley, and I thought if they came to William's, they'd sing *there*, and I could play for them. Only they—"

"—Are more interested in the newspaper," Miss Hodges supplied. "Right now, at least."

"Yes ma'am."

"Louretta, you don't have to call me 'ma'am,' " the teacher corrected gently. " 'Ma'am' is servant talk. You're much too smart to be a servant when you grow up."

"Oh, yes, ma'am," Louretta said, and bit her tongue.

Miss Hodges smiled at this and said, "Well, this presents a lot of problems. First of all, I don't know whether your friends will want me at their meeting. They may resent my presence. After all, it's *their* newspaper."

"Yes, ma'am," Louretta said automatically.

Miss Hodges made a mock-sour face. "Secondly, I'm not sure what you're asking me to do. Do you really want me to help your friends with the newspaper, or do you want me to help you switch them from writing to music?"

Louretta's quick temper made her forget to say "ma'am" this time. "Well, why can't we have both?"

"I don't know. Maybe you can." Miss Hodges' smile was brief. "You say it's your brother William's printing shop. How does *he* feel about all this?"

61

"I don't know, Miss Hodges. See—he always wanted to be a printer, even though Momma was against it, and I was the one who told him about the building for rent, and he was grateful, so he let me bring the kids there. But now that they're there, I think he's worried."

"I don't wonder," Miss Hodges said. "You're worried too, Louretta. I can tell. It looks like you and William have got yourselves a tiger by the tail, and now you want someone to help you with it."

"A tiger by the tail?"

"Something bigger than you can handle."

"Yes, ma'am."

"I do wish you could break that habit," Miss Hodges said. "Otherwise you'll still be saying 'ma'am' when you're forty years old." She took a deep breath and let it out with a sigh. "Oh, well. There are worse habits, I guess. When do you want me to come, Louretta?"

"Today, Miss Hodges. Right after school."

"Oh, Louretta," Miss Hodges complained. She looked at her watch again. "Do you realize what I have to do this evening? Meet my friend for dinner, then visit my sick mother at the hospital, then go home and mark a hundred and twenty papers. I'll be lucky if I even get any sleep tonight."

"Yes, ma'am," Louretta said dully. She turned to go.

"I'll think about it, Louretta. I really will. And I'll try to come sometime. But I doubt if I can make it today."

Louretta did not even bother to look back or say good-by. She spent most of the next hour and a half sitting on the low wall beside the school steps and staring into space. Finally she found herself headed toward home, groaning like an old woman because she was stiff and sore from sitting on cold stone.

Momma had an angry glare in her eye when Louretta walked in. "Well, I hope you're satisfied," she said.

"What do you mean, Momma?"

"I mean you and your brother got your heads together, and you talked him into renting that place, and it's going to be the ruin of this family."

"She means William took a day off from work today," Arneatha volunteered from the couch where she was reading a *Screen Stars* magazine.

"Well, what's so bad about that?" Louretta wanted to know. "*You* haven't gone to work in four weeks."

Arneatha made a smacking sound with her tongue and teeth, indicating that she didn't care what Louretta thought about her work habits, and went back to her magazine.

"Why worry, Momma?" Louretta said. "William told me last month he had twenty-two days of sick leave coming. Why shouldn't he use one of them to get his shop ready?"

"Because he's got no business *having* a shop, that's why," Momma said. "Not if it means taking time off from that good job. He'll take a day off here, a day off there, and the first thing you know, he'll get fired."

"You worry too much, Momma." For once Louretta and Arneatha said the same thing at the same time.

"I have to worry. I have to see that you all get fed. Besides," she added to Louretta, "I went around there a

63

little while ago, and William wasn't getting a bit of work done. The place was packed with those friends of yours. Jitterbugs and hoodlums."

Louretta was hurt. It seemed everybody had a bad opinion of her friends. "I don't know why you blame me for everything William does," she said. "He's grown, and I'm only fourteen."

"Women are *born* grown. Men are always little boys," Momma declared. "You ought to know that."

"That's exactly what's wrong with the way you treat William!" Louretta shouted, and then, because Momma was bearing down on her with vengeance in her eye, edged toward the door. "I'm going around the corner too. I can see I'm not wanted here."

Momma came closer and put a firm hand under Louretta's chin, lifting it so that Louretta was forced to stare into her mother's calm, clear eyes. "Now look here, Missy, I got a look at some of those fellows you call your friends today. Big, ugly, mean-looking boys, some of them. I don't want you messing around with boys like that. I don't want one of them giving me another grandchild."

Louretta squirmed away from her mother. "Momma, I'm going. You can't stop me. But you don't have to worry. William's there. He won't let anything happen to me. Not that it would anyway. The trouble is, you don't have any faith in your children."

"My children are human. They can make mistakes," Momma said. "I only have faith in the Lord." But after a long, hard look, she let Louretta go.

Then pray, Momma, Louretta thought as she ran

out of the house. *Pray that things turn out all right.* Because, to tell the truth, she had some doubts of her own.

The sign, in gleaming gold letters, was completed:

> *The Cheerful*
> *Printing Press*
> *Wm. Hawkins, Prop.*

But Calvin, applying the finishing touches to his handiwork, looked worried. "How's it look?" he asked.

"Beautiful, Calvin. Only—"

Calvin hurled the bottle to the ground, where it spilled a stream of gold along the sidewalk to the gutter. "I knew it!" he cried. "It isn't good enough. My letters don't match up with the old ones. Isn't that what you were going to say?"

"No, it wasn't," Louretta said calmly. She bent, picked up the bottle and handed it to him. "Here. Before it all spills.

"Your letters are perfect, Calvin. I was only going to say, I wish William would let us call it The Cheerful *Clubhouse* and Printing Press."

"Oh," Calvin said. He scowled at her for another few seconds, then let his shy smile appear from behind the clouds. "As long as you think it's all right."

Louretta didn't know why her opinion meant so much to him, but she was pleased. "I think it's beautiful, Calvin."

"Maybe he'll let me do some murals on the walls, too," he said eagerly. "I have some ideas. I worked up a sketch that shows the history of printing."

Louretta didn't want to say anything to discourage this strange, intense boy. "Maybe he will, after he sees what a good job you've done on the window. But he might be too busy to think about it right now."

"Yeah, I guess you're right. He's got his hands full today, with all those kids and teachers in there."

"Teachers? What teachers?"

"They were looking for you. They said you asked them to come."

Louretta wanted to ask Calvin to go inside with her, but he had returned to staring fiercely and critically at his sign. He would not leave it until he was satisfied, so she went in alone.

There was bedlam in the back room, but little Miss Hodges was quieting it down and taking control, the way she did in her classes. After clapping her hands for attention, she said, "I'm only here because one of you asked me to come. And I won't stay unless you want me to."

"Good," Fess said rudely. Several of the boys cheered, and Jethro piped up, "We see enough teachers all day long."

"I know exactly how you feel," Miss Hodges said with a tight little smile. "This is *your* project, after all. I don't intend to interfere. All I want to do is sit and listen."

"I guess we can let her do *that*," Ulysses said reluctantly.

"Thank you," Miss Hodges said. "I do have one suggestion, though. Why don't we take the newspaper meeting upstairs, so William can get his work done?"

"But the press is down here," someone objected.

"Surely you're not going to go to press *today*," Miss

Hodges said. "I understand you're just getting started on the paper."

"Who told you so much about it?" Fess asked suspiciously.

Louretta held her breath until Miss Hodges said, "One of your group. I'd rather not say which one, if you don't mind."

William spoke up. "I'd be mighty grateful if you fellows would go upstairs, like she said. I don't have room to work in here, and I can't think with your meeting going on."

Fess resumed command. "Okay, you guys. Let's have the meeting upstairs. She can come along if she wants. Even though I didn't plan to let any women in on this thing." He gave Louretta a hard look. "I'll bet it was some female who invited her here."

Miss Hodges ignored this comment and made an announcement. "Just one more thing. If any of you want to do some singing, Mr. Lucitanno was kind enough to come here with me today. He's waiting at the piano."

As she passed Louretta, following the rush of boys to the stairs, the teacher winked and whispered, "I decided this was more important than my dinner date."

Louretta wanted to run after her and thank her, but she didn't want Fess to know his guess was right—not yet, anyway. Without knowing why, she was slightly afraid of him. Perhaps it was because he was constantly judging her and deciding that she did not measure up to his standards. She at least wanted to find out what those standards were before she tried to defend herself.

Chords drew Louretta toward the piano instead. A

young, olive-skinned man with a mop of curly black hair was sitting there. It was a minute before Louretta recognized him as the music teacher from Southern High. Mr. Lucitanno's playing was smooth, easy and professional; it made the piano sound much better than Louretta's had. But it was not the way she hoped to play. Something—she did not know what—was missing.

It was, however, attractive enough to draw several boys downstairs. Jethro arrived first, followed by Frank and David, and, later, Ulysses.

"Music is more my stick than writing," Jethro explained. " 'Specially when there's English teachers around. What we gonna sing, Pops? A little 'Jeannie with the Light Brown Hair'?"

The sarcasm in Jethro's voice escaped Mr. Lucitanno. "If you want, yes," he said, completely serious.

"Oh, Lord, de*liv*er us," Jethro complained when Mr. Lucitanno played the first few bars of "Jeannie."

The teacher stopped playing and turned to stare at the boy who was having a fit of giggles in front of him. "Whatever you like, then," he said with an open-handed gesture.

But Jethro, dancing on his toes in merriment, was too convulsed with laughter to suggest anything.

The music teacher turned to Frank and David. "Any suggestions for songs, boys?" Their faces were blank. They remained silent as Calvin, apparently satisfied with his sign at last, appeared in the doorway.

William stuck his head out of the back room. "Hey," he called, "where've all my helpers gone? I didn't mean to chase *everybody* out. I need somebody to help me get out these menus."

"I'm your boy," Calvin responded, with a fierce glance in Louretta's direction. "The rest of you can mess around the piano all day if you want. Me, I'm going to *learn* something."

Oh, Lord, Louretta thought as he disappeared into the back room, *he's angry again.* In spite of her concern she was happy. An hour ago she had been too discouraged to come to the building at all, but now that she was here, she was being pulled in three exciting directions at once. She wanted simultaneously to be upstairs with Miss Hodges, down here with the singers, and in back with William and that strange, fierce new boy. Louretta's love of music had nothing to do with her final decision to stay where she was. She stayed because upstairs she would have to cope with her fear of Fess, while in the back room she might suffer an attack of shyness which William would be quick to spot as a new subject for teasing.

"Maybe *we* can learn something too," Mr. Lucitanno suggested. "We can learn a song."

He played a flowery introduction, then threw back his head and sang:

> There is a lady sweet and kind,
> Was never face so pleased my mind.
> I did but see her passing by,
> And yet I love her till I die.

The song was sweet, but terribly old-fashioned, Louretta thought. The boys listened politely, without expressions on their faces, the way they listened to lessons in school.

"Got that, boys?" Mr. Lucitanno asked eagerly. "Now you try it. You, too, young lady."

He struck his first chord, hitting a jangling sour note. Jethro hooted. Louretta gave him a fierce look, and he hid his remaining giggles in his hand.

"I must get a piano tuner down here," Mr. Lucitanno said seriously. "Now, are we ready? Take it nice and slow. One—two—three—"

They tried. They really tried. But they stumbled in several places, and at the end, they were not together.

"Patience, patience," Mr. Lucitanno said. "All we need is a little more practice."

"Practice won't do it," Frank said. "Excuse me, sir, but it's got no beat. I keep listening for the beat, and it just ain't there."

"Besides," Ulysses asked plaintively, "what do it *mean?* How can you sing a song if it don't mean nothin'?"

"You dummy," said Jethro, whose quick mind had already grasped the meaning of the song and rejected it. "It's about some dumb cat who sees a chick go by his house one time and decides he's in love with her for life. Even though he never sees her again."

"Well how he know she so sweet and kind, if he never even *talked* to her?" Ulysses wanted to know. "She might be the meanest chick in the world, for all he know."

"Well, that's what the song says," Jethro said.

"Pretty dumb, if you ask me," Ulysses said. Then he caught sight of Mr. Lucitanno's disturbed face. "Oh, excuse me, sir. It's a good song."

70

"No, no, don't say it if you don't mean it," the teacher replied. "This is your place, so here you can say anything you want. And *sing* anything you want, too. Now, how about singing me something you like? I will try to follow on the piano."

The boys looked at each other uncertainly until Louretta suggested, "Why don't you sing *Party All Night*? It sounded great the other day in the alley."

Jethro considered this idea, decided he didn't like it, and darted out the door instead. The other boys shrugged— they were used to his sudden impulses—and formed a semicircle. David took the lead while the others sang the refrain, patting their feet and clapping their hands to keep the rhythm:

> Got no money, Jack,
>> Party all night
> Got a pain in my back,
>> Party all night
> Got a pain in my head,
>> Party all night
> Haven't been to bed,
>> Party all night
> But I'm not quite dead!
>> Party all night
> Let's party all, party all, party all night!
>
> Party all night
>> Hang a sign downstairs,
> Party all night
>> Bring some extra chairs,
> Party all night

If they're broke or bent,
Party all night
Charge an extra cent,
Party all night
'Cause we gotta pay the rent!
Let's party all, party all, party all night!

If the landlord knocks,
Party all night
Give him rye on the rocks,
Party all night
If the preacher calls it sin,
Party all night
Give him lots of gin,
Party all night
And invite them both right in!
Party all night
So we can party all, party all, party all night!
Party all night
Till the cows come home . . .

The speed and volume built up steadily until Mr. Lucitanno gave up his attempt to accompany the boys. He took his hands from the keys and just sat there, head cocked to one side, listening intently. When the boys noticed that he had stopped playing, they stopped singing, cutting out raggedly, one by one, and looking ashamed.

But the teacher was pleased. "Amazing!" he exclaimed. "The effects you get without any instruments. How I wish I could accompany you. But I don't know how."

"Here's a guy who can show you," Jethro called from the doorway.

Everyone turned to stare. The grizzled old man Jethro was leading toward them had not had a haircut or a shave in months. He wore several layers of tattered clothes and carried a white cane and a battered guitar case. Louretta, who had seen the old blind man singing and begging on the Avenue, was embarrassed that Jethro had chosen to bring him here today.

But it was too late. Clinging to Jethro's arm, the shabby old man advanced toward the piano, his right hand stuck out in front of him. "Blind Eddie Bell's the name," he said, "and music is my game. Formerly with Jimmy Lunceford, Erskine Hawkins, and Ray Johnson's Little Raiders."

"Pleased to meet you," the teacher said, and shook hands. "I'm Al Lucitanno." He got up to make room on the piano bench.

Blind Eddie played a few notes and chords, then chuckled, "This piano's almost as old as me," he said, "but I guess there's still plenty of music left in both of us."

And without a pause he launched into a lecture that Louretta would never forget. It was a mixture of talking, singing and playing that amounted to a short history of the music and musicians Blind Eddie had known in his long lifetime.

"Blind Lemon Jefferson used to play this one," he said. "I first heard it in Chicago, in the twenties."

Louretta liked the song, about a man out of work and his need for money, even though it was played in an old-fashioned style she had never heard before.

73

"Now, this was Victoria Spivey's most famous number."

"Black Snake Blues" was not a hymn—far from it. It was a very down-to-earth song about a woman who thought another woman was using magic to get her husband away from her, but its rhythm gave Louretta the same feeling of happy excitement as the lively church music she had heard coming from this very building.

Blind Eddie sang next:

> Woke up this morning,
> Blues all around my head.
> Woke up this morning,
> Blues all around my head.
> Went to eat my breakfast,
> Found the same thing in my bread.

"Sonny Terry sings that," he explained, "but it ain't just *his* song. Blues like that belongs to everybody."

Next Blind Eddie played a very familiar tune. "You all know this one, by the late, great W. C. Handy. *Everybody* knows this one. Come on and sing along with me."

"That's right," he said encouragingly, as Ulysses and Frank joined in on "St. Louis Blues." "Sing it from your hearts, now." Louretta soon found herself singing too.

"Hey, that little girl has a great big voice!" Blind Eddie exclaimed when they had finished. "And I didn't even know she was here. Now, this here is one of Fats Waller's numbers."

Louretta hated to interrupt, but she had a terribly important question. "Excuse me. Those musicians you mentioned. Are they all colored?"

74

"Why, sure," Blind Eddie said with an easy laugh. "White people don't write music like this. This is something the colored people done all by themselves."

Louretta felt a warm thrill of pride. "Something the colored people done all by themselves . . ." She wished she had known about this the day of the argument with Donna.

Suddenly she no longer minded Blind Eddie's long hair and ragged clothes. She sat down beside him on the piano bench and said, "Will you show me how to play the blues the way you do?"

"Sure, little girl," Blind Eddie said. "The blues is easy. All you need to know is three chords, and you can play 'most any blues. These are the three chords." And he showed her.

"Blues are too square for me," Jethro remarked, annoyed at Blind Eddie's taking time out to teach Louretta. "That's country music. I'm a city boy."

"But, sonny," Blind Eddie said, "that song you boys were singing when I came in here, that was a blues too. She can play it with those same three chords. Watch."

And, placing Louretta's hands on the keys, he played and sang,

> Got no money, Jack,
> Party all night
> Got a pain in my back,
> Party all night
> Got a pain in my head . . .

The boys joined in and ran through the entire number. Midway through the second chorus, Blind Eddie took his hands away, and Louretta finished playing the song by herself, ending with a flourish of all three chords.

Mr. Lucitanno said, "I had no idea it was so simple."

"It's simple," Blind Eddie said, "but it ain't easy."

"I see what you mean," the teacher said thoughtfully. "It's the feeling that counts."

"That's right," Blind Eddie agreed. "This kind of music, it has to come from the heart, and from living a certain kind of life. A hard life, where people got no chance for kidding themselves, and what little happiness they have, they make it themselves, so they're really glad about it. That's the kind of life colored people has, and that's why they make up the blues."

Mr. Lucitanno was silent.

"Say, listen," Blind Eddie apologized to him, "I hope you don't mind me taking over. I know *you're* supposed to be the teacher."

"Not at all," Mr. Lucitanno said. He hesitated, then broke into an embarrassed, likable grin. "That is—well, I minded a little bit at first, but now I'm glad. I learned something new today."

"Good," Blind Eddie concluded. "Well, it's getting close to my dinnertime. I guess we'd best wind up this session with a church song. At the end of a day I think it always pays to remember the Lord. Besides, the church music came first, and all the other music we were playing came afterward.

"Now, all the words of this hymn are in the title, and it's called "God Be With You Until We Meet Again." And,

little lady, I play it with the same three chords—boom—
boom—boom—like this."

Eddie sang the hymn through once, and then the rest
of them joined in:

> God be with you,
> God be with you,
> God be with you until we meet again.
> God be with you,
> God be with you,
> God be with you until we meet again.

When they finished it seemed as if at least twenty people had been singing. The big empty room echoed with the
resonance of their voices on the final chord, which contained at least eight notes.

Louretta was the first to look around and see that they
had gathered an audience, including William, Miss Hodges
and most of the boys from the newspaper meeting upstairs.
Some of them must have been singing along.

"I guess," Jethro said with mock sadness, "no matter
what we do to it, this place will always be a church."

"Don't knock it, man," Fess said. "I don't dig praying
and all that nonsense, but that music really has soul."

Louretta was slowly acquiring a dim understanding
of what he meant by his favorite term of approval. "Soul"
was something deep and moving which she was beginning
to recognize because something in her always rushed out to
meet it.

They were all sorry when Blind Eddie rose and picked
up his shabby guitar case. Tapping his way to the door, he

said, "I'll be back if you want me to play for you some more."

"Come back tomorrow!" David cried.

"Come back *every day!*" Louretta called.

Though no one had asked him, Mr. Lucitanno said, "I will be back tomorrow too."

SIX

MOMMA'S GLOOMY WARNINGS AND WILLIAM'S WORRIED SI-
lences had no effect on Louretta that week. Nothing could
bring her down from the cloud of happiness she had inhab-
ited ever since Blind Eddie Bell had opened the door to a
new world of music and handed her the key. Every day after school Eddie helped her with blues chords, teaching her
variations and giving her new examples from the treasure-
chest of music that filled his gray head:

*The key you pick is important, little lady. Your voice
sounds best in G. That's good, 'cause G is a happy key. B
flat is sort of a sad key, and C minor is even sadder. . . ."*

Every night after supper she rushed back to the building to practice what she had learned that afternoon.

But tonight things were not going so well. After only
a week of listening to Blind Eddie and practicing, she had
learned to be dissatisfied with the sounds that had delighted
her so when she first produced them. She could play the
simple chords, yes, but Blind Eddie could do so much more
with them—little ripples, unexpected changes of key, and
extra notes with amazing power. A single extra note could
make a chord sound twice as rich. She wasn't sure she had

the rhythm right, either. It was so much easier to keep the rhythm when Blind Eddie was at her side, humming the tune and patting his feet on the floor. Determined to improve, she tried once more, singing softly as she played:

> I got a girl
> On the other side of town.
> I got a girl
> Other side of town.
> She picks me up
> When the others let me down.
>
> This girl I mean,
> Her name is Sally Ann.
> This girl I mean,
> Her name is Sally Ann.
> And if you can't help me,
> Well, I know she can.

She was rollicking along, feeling good about the music, beginning to believe she might have the knack of it after all, when a shattering laugh came out of the shadows. Louretta stopped playing and peered into the darkness.

The hooting laugh was repeated. "What makes you think you can learn to play blues? Something like that can't be learned. You either born with it, or you ain't."

She was so absorbed in her playing that she had not noticed how dark it was getting. The shadows were impossible to penetrate, and she could not identify the voice.

"Gal like you singing the blues, that's as ridiculous as J. Edgar Hoover doin' the boogaloo." The unearthly, hooting chuckle floated out of a different corner this time.

Louretta felt a clutch of fear: it might be a prowler, a burglar, anyone who had wandered in off the street. Then the lights of a passing car flashed on the lenses of a pair of round spectacles.

Louretta got up and felt her way to the wall switch. She was always at a disadvantage with this boy, but she could at least eliminate the extra handicap of not being able to see him. "If you don't like it, you don't have to listen," she said calmly, and flicked on the naked hanging bulb to reveal Fess squatting in one corner, ugly and grouchy as a toad.

The light made him much less frightening. "Why do you always have to be against everything?" she asked with sudden courage. "And what have you got against *me*, anyway?"

"What makes you think I've got something against you, Miss Priss?" he shot back.

"That's what I mean. You can't even talk to me without insulting me. I was just sitting here enjoying myself, not bothering you at all."

"You were insulting my ears," he growled. "What you were doing sounded like what white musicians do to our music. All the surface and none of the soul."

His criticism hurt because she knew there was some truth in it—she had already recognized a frustrating deficiency in her reproductions of Blind Eddie's music—but she defended herself anyway.

"But I'm not white."

"Almost," he snapped. "Have you looked at yourself lately?"

"A person's color is not their fault," she replied, and added without thinking, "Do I blame you because you're ugly?"

He flinched and seemed to be trying to grow smaller inside his skin, but Louretta was past caring about his feelings. "That's why you're so mean and evil. You're mad cause you're so ugly. If you acted nicer, people would forget you're not nice-looking. For a smart boy you're pretty dumb if you don't know a simple thing like that."

With a single great bound—more and more he reminded her of a frog—Fess leaped to his feet from his squatting position and started toward the door. He carried himself stiffly, as if he'd been wounded. Once again Louretta regretted not having held her tongue. But he was much too proud to accept an apology. Noticing a bundle of papers under his arm, she seized on them instead.

"What've you got there? Stories for the newspaper?"

"Yeah," came the muffled answer from deep in his throat.

Having scored her victory, Louretta was eager to make amends. "Oh, let me see them. Please. I'm dying to read them."

"You wouldn't understand," he croaked. But he had stopped walking, and had half turned back toward her.

Louretta was carefully humble. "I'll try my best," she said. "I know I'm not very smart about the race problem and things like that. But if I don't understand, maybe you'll be kind enough to explain it to me."

Behind the thick glasses, his eyes lifted to hers in an unbelieving stare. "Here," he said, and stiffly held out a handful of papers.

"RESIST RACIST COPS!!!!!" said the first page, with five exclamation points beside the headline. Louretta only got through the beginning of the first paragraph:

> An armed monster stalks our community. Big, beefy, with a red neck and a blue uniform, he beats up our women and children and shoots down young men on sight. His brain is as small as the rest of him is large—he usually wears size 2 hats and size 12 shoes. Yet this moron has ABSOLUTE POWER over us unless we do something about him! Unless we fight back against this monster, we deserve all the suffering he causes us. . . .

Louretta looked up from the page. "You write very well," she said timidly.

"Thanks," he said shortly.

"But," she added, "don't you think you've exaggerated things a little?"

"Every word there is true," he said, staring stonily at a point on the wall a couple of feet to the right of her. "I go on to give examples to prove my point. Real ones, from the newspapers."

"Oh, I know it's *true*," she hedged. "I mean, I know the cops are mean. Some of them. But they don't all have big feet and little heads. Some of them are in proportion." She was tempted to giggle.

"This is a *symbolic* cop I'm writing about!" he shouted. "A mixture of all the cops I've known." He made an impatient gesture, as if talking to her were a waste of time. "Details don't matter, anyway. The point is to get the message across."

"Yes, but suppose one day a person sees a normal-looking cop. Or one who has little *feet* and a big *head*. And maybe a neck that isn't red at all, but white or brown. Then suppose, that same day, that same person reads this article. He might think, 'This writer's little facts aren't right, so his *big* facts can't be right either.' "

"I told you you wouldn't understand." Fess held out his hand for the papers.

"Wait, there's something else here I want to read," she said, looking through them quickly.

"You won't understand that either. Give them all back."

"No, wait, Fess," she pleaded. "Let me look at this. I've heard so much about your poetry, and I've never had a chance to read any of it."

"All right, but hurry up," he growled, and turned his back, hands stuffed deep in his pockets.

Louretta suspected that he cared more about his poems than about his other writing, and resolved not to criticize the poem even if she disliked it as much as the article. But her resolution wasn't necessary.

"It's great, Fess!" she cried after she finished. "Oh, I hope you *do* print the newspaper. And I hope you put this on the front page."

He gave her his amazed pop-eyed stare again. "You really mean it?"

"I wish I could write something half as good," she said sincerely.

Still not quite believing her, he said with jerky gestures, "Look, maybe you don't get it. It's not just a cat poem. It's about a man who—"

She interrupted quickly. "It's a good poem, it doesn't need explaining."

"It needs some revising," he said uncomfortably.

"Oh, no, it's perfect the way it is. I hope you won't change a single word."

Fess shuffled awkwardly in place, as if her praise disturbed him more than her criticism had, and thrust out his hand for the papers.

Louretta gave them all back except the poem. "I want to ask a favor. Will you let me keep this, Fess? Just for one night? Please."

He was startled and suspicious. "What for?"

She started to tell him the truth, then thought better of it. "I want to memorize it," she lied. "Whenever I find something I really like, I try to commit it to memory."

He was still giving her that unbelieving stare, so she went on, "My mother taught me to do that. She used to make us memorize Bible verses. That way, she said, no one can ever take them away from us."

"That's what's wrong with our folks now. All that religion," he said, "If they ever got up off their knees they might be able to hold up their heads."

"You may be right," she said meekly, and thought of what Momma would say. *That boy's a devil. You're as bad as the Devil yourself, if you listen to what he says and don't denounce him.* But instead of denouncing him, she merely smiled at the thought of Momma's reaction. "I like to memorize poetry mostly now. I'd love to memorize your poem."

"Well, suit yourself," he said gruffly. At the door he had an afterthought. "As long as you don't show it to that teacher friend of yours. I don't want her to see it till it's ready."

"I won't," she promised, but smiled to herself. Perhaps Fess was less fierce and independent than he seemed, if he was planning to submit his writings to Miss Hodges.

She was much less frightened of him now, but she was still glad to see him go. She'd been eager for him to leave ever since the exciting idea had first occurred to her. *Hungry Cat Blues.* A poem with a title like that should be set to music!

She started off very slowly, searching for the chords one at a time. Composing a song was like building a house, Blind Eddie said; first you found the chords, which were the building blocks, and then you stretched the melody across them like a row of planks. At last she had found the chords for the first three lines:

> I'm a hungry cat,
> Walkin' by my lonesome,
> All alone and blue.

But the next line was harder; this was not a simple three- or four-line blues, like most of the songs Blind Eddie knew. It was more complicated. She felt her way slowly, playing false chord after false chord, feeling blinder than the old blind musician, because he at least could see where he was going on a piano. What was needed was a shift in key, something told her—but which key? She did not know. After many trials and mistakes, she found the next chords:

> Ain't got no money, boys.
> Ain't got a darn thing to do.

Louretta had a feeling of enormous satisfaction when she finished setting the first five lines to music. She played and sang them over several times, and liked the results better each time. But there were two more lines in the first verse, and she hadn't the faintest idea of what to do with them. She tried chord after chord, and none of them sounded right. They didn't have the coming-to-an-end feeling that belonged at the end of a verse. After a dozen tries she gave up and played the beginning over again:

> I'm a hungry cat,
> Walkin' by my lonesome . . .

Suddenly she had it! The missing chords had been right there all the time. The end of the verse needed to return to the same key as the beginning:

> All alone and blue,
> And my woman's left me too.

The first verse sounded exactly right to her ears as she played it through. With mounting excitement, she went right into the chorus. The chorus was easy; its four lines fit perfectly with the three basic chords Blind Eddie had taught her:

(First chord)   Now, the white cat drinks double-A rich milk,
(Second chord) The yellow cat sleeps on a bed of silk.
(First chord)   The brown cat's better off than me.
(Third chord) I'm black and got nothin' but misery.

And there it was—an entire song from Fess's poem! It was not a "pretty little flower poem" at all. (How little Fess really knew her!) It was an angry poem, and an even angrier song, but it was true, and she liked it. She sang it through once more, leaning steadily on the loud pedal and letting her voice come from deep in her chest.

"Well, now, who have we got here?" said a voice at her elbow. "Bessie Smith in person? Or is it Little Esther, up way past her bedtime?"

She jumped and turned to look up the long, long height of her brother. These days, his smiles were not broad enough to erase the permanent worry lines. "Sorry, Brother Bill. I didn't mean to bother you."

"It's not me I'm worried about, it's the neighbors. You were getting so loud they could hear you way across town. Where are all your friends?"

"Gone home, I guess." She had lost track of the time. It must be late, though; nearly eleven o'clock.

"And that's where you ought to be too. Home in bed or doing your homework. I had no idea you were still here."

There was no comfortable place at home for doing homework, and she didn't want to go to bed because one of the twins had begun wetting the bed every night, and Momma simply didn't have enough sheets to change them every day. The whole house smelled bad, for that matter, in spite of Momma's constant scrubbing, because there were just too many people in it. She didn't mention any of these things to William, though. He had to live there too, and he had enough problems.

Instead she said, "I forgot about the time," and helped him clean up the back room and lock the building. Then they walked together up the bright, busy Avenue, which was so noisy Louretta could not imagine anyone objecting to her singing. There were people on the Avenue who never seemed to go to bed. Perhaps, like Louretta, they did not like the beds that were waiting for them.

"Say, I never knew my little sis had such a great big voice," William said. "Maybe you're going to be the famous one in the family."

"As well as the smart one and the pretty one," she teased.

"That will do, Sister Lou," he warned, and squeezed her hand until it hurt. He added, "I should've known the piano was the reason why you wanted me to rent that building so bad. You were dying for a piano all along."

Louretta wasn't talking. She was too busy singing—not out loud, but inside. The song in her head grew steadily louder until it drowned out her thoughts. Deep in her pockets, her hands were busy too, playing chords on an imaginary keyboard. Each time she sang the song over in her mind, it sounded better. She could hardly wait to play it for the gang tomorrow and learn Fess's reaction. Would he like it? She hoped so. There was a good chance. After all, he had written the words!

Though Louretta carefully folded a blanket and spread it on the floor and lay down on it as soon as she got home, she was a long time getting to sleep that night. And in the morning her fingers were the stiffest part of her body, and her throat was aching and sore as if she had spent the night singing.

SEVEN

"WE'RE GOING TO TRY SOMETHING DIFFERENT THIS WEEK," Miss Hodges told the class. "Instead of a book report or an essay on an assigned topic, I want you to choose your own subjects. Write an essay or a story or a poem about something that is important to you. If you can't do an essay or a story, write a letter to a friend. If you haven't got a friend, write a letter to me."

This last comment drew laughter from around the room; apparently they all had plenty of friends, except Louretta.

"Now, what are some of the subjects we might write about? Florence?"

"The most wonderful person I've ever known," Florence said.

"Good, Florence. Work on that. What are you going to write about, Louretta?"

Louretta, half asleep and thinking of other things, had not been paying very careful attention. "Uh—my mother. She's a pretty wonderful person."

The teacher was disappointed. "I was hoping you'd come up with a different idea, Louretta. I don't want everyone to pick the same topics. And class—there are no limits on the subjects you can write about. Anything that's important to you."

Jethro's hand was in the air, waving agitatedly. "How about sex, Miss Hodges?"

Miss Hodges frustrated Jethro's attempt to embarrass her by embarrassing him instead. "Certainly. Just make sure you know what you're writing about, Jethro."

After three minutes of laughter, the room came alive with buzzes of whispered conversation. Even Joella waved an eager hand.

"I saw a murder on my street last month, Miss Hodges. This boy, he was just walking along, and another boy come out of the alley and shot him. There was blood all over the place, and the boy's mother fainted and had to go to the hospital. Can I write about the murder?"

"Of course, Joella. Make us see it as vividly as you did. Make us care about the boy who died. Yes, Henry?"

"What about a story about somebody who has to go to church twice a week but doesn't believe in God?"

"Write it, Henry," Miss Hodges said. "That's the kind of thing I want. After the papers are all in, I may have a surprise for you. There is a chance that the best ones will be published."

The class, which normally hated to write, began wielding pencils as if their lives depended on it, while usually eager Louretta lagged behind. She wrote across the top of the page:

The Most Wonderful Person I've Ever Known
My Mother

At the end of the hour she had written nothing more. But the page was covered with doodles—a cat, a pair of round horn-rimmed glasses, a number of quarter and half notes, and a piano keyboard with black and white keys stretching across the page.

She reached the shabby building on the Avenue before the other kids, before the teachers, before William, even. She had to wait for her brother to arrive with the keys.

"Don't know what to do about you, Sister Lou," he said. "You're the first to arrive in the daytime and the last one to leave at night. How are you coming on with your schoolwork?"

"Fine," she lied.

"Well, tonight don't come back here after dinner. Stay home and do some homework," he ordered.

She readily agreed; she only wanted a couple of hours at the piano anyway. Her happiness was complete when the first arrival turned out to be Blind Eddie. The old man had nothing to do all day, so late every afternoon he drew near the building and waited for signs of life. Louretta practically dragged him to the piano.

"Listen, Eddie, and tell me what you think of this song." She played and sang the first verse and chorus while the old man listened and smiled.

"Do you like it?" she asked him.

"Sho," he said. "That's a real fine number. It has a message. Where'd you learn it?"

"I wrote it," she said proudly. "That is, one of the fellows wrote the words. Fess. You know Fess?" He nodded. "And I wrote the music."

"Well, now, I'm real proud of you. For somebody who

just learned the chords a week ago, you're doing real good. If you'll just let old Eddie give you a few tips . . ."

Though he had only heard the song once, he played through it rapidly, improving her efforts as he went along. "Play a bass like this, little lady, it helps the singer keep the rhythm. . . . Give that C chord a flatted seventh the second time you play it; that's what makes it sound like the blues. . . . And before each verse, you might drag your finger down the high keys up here, to make a sound like a cat meowing. . . . No, wait, I can do it better on my guitar."

Handling the old man's only treasure carefully, she helped him get it out of the case and sling it around his neck. When the first of the boys arrived, Louretta and Blind Eddie were both singing lustily and playing:

> You know a hungry cat
> Ain't got time for nothin'
> But findin' food to eat.
> He don't want friendly talk
> When he visits on your street.
> When he strolls down your street,
> What he's lookin' for is meat!

The verses were there for all to read on the piano. Ulysses and Frank needed no prompting to join in:

> You better leave some seafood at my door.
> Add a little sirloin to be sure,
> Plus a quart of heavy cream,
> Or I'll come around and smash your dream.

Soon another voice was added to the chorus—Calvin's. That moody young artist consented to abandon the serious business of the print shop long enough to sing the last verse:

> 'Cause I can move real fast,
> Jump out in the darkness,
> And run and not be seen.
> You better treat me right,
> Or you'll find out what I mean.
> If I can't be rich,
> I can sure be mean!

"Yeah!" came a shout of endorsement from the end of the piano, where a large group stood.

"Now there's a song makes some sense," Ulysses approved.

"Yeah," David put in. "I think it's cool. It starts out about a cat, but it's really about a man."

"Well, people call a man a 'cat' sometimes," said one of the girls.

"It's about *both*, stupid!" Jethro yelled at the others. "A cat *and* a man. It's about both of 'em. That's why it's so cool."

Blind Eddie made the final comment. "It's about *life*. And there ain't no lies in it, which is why it's true."

The door opened again, and Louretta looked around eagerly, hoping Fess had arrived and would hear his poem sung. But no light came through the door. It was blocked by a mountain of blue.

His neck *was* red, she observed dully as Officer Lafferty turned to call something to his partner in the car parked at the curb, and his feet did seem awfully big. But then *all* of him was awfully big.

94

"All right, what are you kids doing in here?"

"We were just singing," Louretta told him.

"Well, keep the noise down," The Man ordered. "We've got enough trouble in this neighborhood without all that bellowing."

"Is there a law against singing?" Sharon asked saucily.

"There's a law against disturbing the peace," he informed her, "and I'll damn well enforce it in my district."

Sharon finished her question. "—Or is it just that you can't stand to see people happy?"

A tide of red moved up from Officer Lafferty's neck to his face. With a lumbering movement, he caught Sharon by the shoulder and slammed her against the wall.

"Any of the rest of you want the same treatment, go ahead and get smart like she did," he said.

"She's pregnant. You could have killed her baby!" Louretta screamed.

The policeman looked at Sharon, huddled on the floor against the wall, as if seeing her for the first time. "Well, fine. That'll be one less to deal with when he grows up." Then he grinned, showing uneven, yellowish teeth. "But that's not likely. You colored gals are tough. You're no different from animals."

Louretta was too angry to feel fear. "I was about to say the same thing about you," she said coldly, then sucked in her breath in a spasm of terror, because the huge uniformed Man was coming toward her. Beside her on the bench, Blind Eddie raised his precious guitar as if to ward off blows.

The other boys remained still and silent, frozen with fear, but Calvin swiftly moved to put himself between the cop and Louretta. "You keep your hands off her and that old man," he said to the huge Man. "Hit me instead, if you got to hit somebody."

. The policeman seemed amused. "You want to be a hero, boy? Okay. Let's see how fast you can move out to that patrol car."

And then, because Calvin still stood there, he gave him a prod with his night stick. "I said get out there and get in that car. Now *move!*"

. Louretta squeezed her eyes shut to stop the tears from running down her face. What was happening was all her fault, but there was nothing she could do to help. Calvin obeyed the cop.

"Now, who's in charge here?" Lafferty demanded.

With silent motions of their heads and eyes they pointed to the back room, and Officer Lafferty strode off in the direction they had indicated.

Louretta could not distinguish the words that were spoken back there; she could only hear the officer's strident, threatening voice and William's soft, continuous undertone of pleading. Though the conversation was indistinct, its tendency was clear, and it made her both angry and ashamed. When the tears came back, she let them fall in great wet *plops* on the piano keys.

At last it was over. William called an unnecessary, "I'll see that they behave, Officer," and Lafferty strode out of the building without condescending to look at any of them again. He got in the front seat of the patrol car beside the driver. Calvin, his head bowed, was in back.

"You boys didn't do anything to help," Louretta complained.

96

"You *girls* started the trouble in the first place," was David's cold answer.

"Our women always do that," Blind Eddie commented. "They ain't got enough sense to keep their mouths shut, and then our mens take the blame and go to jail or die for it. There's lots of songs about that situation, like 'Betty and Dupree.' Lots of songs."

Louretta, on the brink of a cataract of tears, sniffled.

"Shut up, you jerks," Jethro hissed fiercely. "Stop talking and sing. Sing, so he'll know we're not scared."

Louretta didn't know whether he meant Lafferty or Calvin, but impressing either of them was sufficient reason to respond immediately. As she played and sang, the tears dried up of their own accord. William came running in to halt the singing, but when he saw his sister's streaked, stony face, he lowered his eyes and slipped away.

When she felt the draft caused by the door's opening again and heard the tread of heavy feet, she did not look around. Beside her Blind Eddie's guitar twanged humorously, and around her the voices of the others surged up to give her courage. The song ended in triumph, and in the reverberating silence that followed, she waited calmly for the heavy hand on her shoulder that would drag her off to jail.

But the next voice she heard was Mr. Lucitanno's, eager and innocent, full of enthusiasm. "Say, that sounded great! What do you call that number?"

"You might call it 'Music to go to jail by,'" Blind Eddie said, and chuckled. Louretta was proud of the old man. He too must have been waiting in dreadful suspense,

97

unable to look around and see who was there. Suddenly released from their tension, all the kids laughed.

"That's real dangerous music," Ulysses remarked. "It brings the cops for an audience."

"I don't understand," the white teacher said. "You mean the police were here?"

"Yes, and they took one of the boys away," Louretta said.

"Which boy?"

"Calvin Ringer," somebody supplied.

"He was a quiet boy. He never bothered anybody. All he was doing was trying to protect me," Louretta said. She found to her shame that she was sniffling moistly again.

Mr. Lucitanno patted her on the shoulder. "Now, now, Louretta. Don't cry."

She jerked away from him. "I'm not crying!" she yelled.

"That's better," he said. "Now, why did they take Calvin away? What happened?"

"Nothing," Louretta said. The others shrugged and were silent.

"Come *on* now," Mr. Lucitanno said with a perplexed look on his handsome, boyish face. "The police don't just walk into places and arrest people without a reason."

But that was exactly what they did all the time in Southside. Louretta despaired of ever being able to explain this to Mr. Lucitanno, though; he had not grown up in Southside. He would not believe her or understand.

"But they don't do that in America. This is a free country!" the teacher shouted. He must be close to thirty, yet he seemed, somehow, younger than any of the group around the piano. No one said anything, and then Jethro laughed—a shrieking, high-pitched, crazy laugh that said Southside was not in America-the-land-of-the-free and never had been.

The teacher blushed dark red under his olive skin. "Well," he said, embarrassed, "it would help if I knew what had happened, but I'll go to the police station anyway and try to get your friend released. But first, will you run through that number again for me? I only heard the end of it."

"She forgot to tell you," Blind Eddie spoke up. "That boy Fess wrote the words, and she wrote the music."

"With Eddie's help," Louretta added.

"Then, by all means, let me hear it."

More for his sake than for their own enjoyment, because they had lost the spirit, they ran through the song again, with David, Frank, Ulysses and Jethro singing, Louretta playing the piano, and Blind Eddie on guitar. The others hummed and clapped their hands.

"Bravo!" Mr. Lucitanno cried when they had finished. "But don't you think it's a little . . . er . . . bitter?"

The faces around the piano were blank.

Mr. Lucitanno coughed. "Well, anyway," he said, "I can see why you don't like eighteenth-century songs."

Jethro spoke for all of them. "Man, I expect to live to the twenty-*first* century. What you expect me to know about some old eighteenth?"

"You have a point," Mr. Lucitanno agreed. "You know, I've been wondering all week how I may be of use to you kids. You don't really need any help with singing.

You are already accomplished singers, and you have your own style and your own tastes. But I think Mr. Bell's guitar added a great deal to that rendition, don't you?"

The group agreed noisily, with cheers and applause for Blind Eddie.

"Then perhaps *other* instruments would add even more. How many of you would like to learn an instrument, so you could *play* as well as sing?"

"Me, man! I want me a horn!" Jethro shouted.

"I want to blow drums," said Walter, a ragged older boy who always rapped professionally on the piano top while they sang.

"A clarinet for me!" said another boy. "A long, fine licorice stick."

"Well, I can teach you to play all those instruments. And I can get any one of them, used, for twenty dollars."

Their faces went gloomy, but Mr. Lucitanno did not seem to notice the change. "You think about it, and let me know which instruments you want to buy. Right now I have to go see the police about Calvin. I'll try to get them to leave you alone after this."

He turned to leave, and almost bumped into Fess, who was just arriving. "Excuse me," Mr. Lucitanno said, "got to get to the police station."

"Fuzz been here?" Fess asked curtly of Frank, his lieutenant.

"Yeah, man," Frank replied, lapsing into tough slang. "They rapped about the noise we was makin', and they hauled one of the cats off to the dungeon."

"Which cat?"

"Calvin."

"We got to spring him," Fess said. He couldn't be serious—he was only a boy, they were *all* only boys—yet he had the grim expression of an experienced warrior. Louretta shivered.

"The dago said *he'd* do it," David supplied.

"Hell, man, don't trust *him*. Don't trust white people to do *anything*. How many times I got to tell you that?" Fess exploded. "What else was the dago puttin' down?"

"Oh, some old stuff about instruments," Jethro said.

"*Instruments?*"

"He like all white people," Ulysses explained with a sad, helpless smile. "He mean well, but he just don't understand. Said he could get us instruments for twenty dollars apiece. Hell, man, my whole family ain't never had twenty dollars at one time in their whole life!"

Everyone laughed, but the laughter had sour overtones.

"I'm thinking," Fess said. He looked up. "How many of you cats want to blow instruments?"

Four hands shot into the air. "Me, man!" "Me!" "Me!"

"That's four of you. That's eighty dollars. Now, this is what I think." Fess dragged a chair over and sat down on it backwards, his arms folded on the chair back. "The gang's been gettin' soft. We ain't had a rumble since last year."

"The Avengers been coolin' it ever since you bopped their leader," David said proudly. "When they heard what you did to LeRoy Smith, they laid off of us."

"Yeah," Jethro put in, "but I heard a rumor they're plannin' to attack again, now we've got this clubhouse."

"You see what I mean?" Fess said. "We gonna have our hands full. The Avengers are gonna be on our backs again, and besides, we're gonna have to fight the cops sooner or later. Today was only the beginning."

The boys were very sober and quiet now.

"We're about to be at war."

Jethro suddenly threw back his head and screamed delightedly, "Good!" It was like an Indian's war cry, and gave Louretta another attack of the shivers.

Fess grinned and looked around. It was an unpleasant grin.

His large, prominent eyes were glittering. "So what I've been thinkin' is, we better tighten up the organization. Get the weapons in shape. And get us a little practice."

"How, man?" Frank asked tensely.

"We gonna *steal* us that eighty dollars."

Jethro was skipping around the room in transports of delight. "I know a place where hub caps bring four bucks apiece. We can pick up twenty dollars in one raid easy. More if we go uptown where the Cadillacs are."

"And we can knock off a store," Frank suggested. "Old Silberman's pawnshop might be a good one. He's so old he won't be no trouble. And he's always got at least fifty in the cash register."

"What's in the arsenal?" Fess asked him.

"Four knives, two zip guns, a .38, and a shotgun."

"Shotgun's no good. Too hard to hide on the street. But get the other weapons ready. And you and Hoss bring 'em here tonight."

They were calling David by his nickname more and more; it was a sign the boys felt he had reached manhood.

102

"What's the plan?" he asked.

"If Calvin ain't sprung, we go down to the police station. If he is, we move on Silberman."

Louretta's hands, which had been trembling for some time, suddenly came down on a dozen piano keys at once. Above the horrendous discord, her voice screamed, "*No!*"

Stunned into silence, they all turned and looked at her. She would never remember exactly what she said or how she said it; all she knew was that she told them, in a strained, high-pitched voice, that they could not use her brother's shop as headquarters for a gang of thieves. On no account could they bring weapons there. And if they were going to reactivate the gang and start fighting again, they could just forget about the clubhouse. She, Louretta, would close it and keep them out.

"Ain't that just like a woman?" Frank commented.

"Don't listen to her," Fess said. "She's just like all those other old Toms who tell us to believe in law and order. The cops just been here kickin' her around today, and she still can't see that the law's against us whether we break it or not. We have to be outlaws. They *make* us outlaws. But she can't see that."

"If we don't steal, how are we gonna get the money for the instruments, Lou?" David asked reasonably.

"I don't know. But if you have to steal, you're better off without them."

"Aaaah," Fess muttered in disgust, "law and order never did nothin' for them old Toms, and they won't do nothing for you either. The only way to get what you want is to take it."

The evil advocated by this boy was beginning to tempt Louretta, which made her more determined than ever to defeat it. She had an inspiration born of desperation. "We could have a dance," she said.

"A *dance!* Awww!" Jethro's loud expression of disgust seemed to speak for most of the boys. But the girls immediately showed interest in the dance as an alternative to Fess's plan. Perhaps it was because it would include them, while gang-fighting and robbery would not.

"This room's big enough for a dance. But it's awfully gloomy," Joella said, looking around.

"We could decorate it with crepe paper from the five and ten," Florence suggested. "And some colored light bulbs would give it a nice atmosphere."

"We could charge seventy-five cents admission," Louretta said, silently praying that her idea would go over. "If only a hundred kids came, we'd make seventy-five dollars."

"We could sell refreshments to make more," Sharon volunteered. "Sodas and hot dogs would be easy."

Fess made another attempt to discourage Louretta. "What are you going to use for music?"

"We can all bring records. My brother William will lend us his machine," she replied quickly, hoping William would make good her promise. "What's more, he'll probably let us print up some posters on his press."

Jethro suddenly switched his point of view. He was just like a little child; his enthusiasm detached itself from one project and attached itself to another very quickly. But he was able to lead the others. "Oh, crazy!" he cried. "We can put up posters all over town."

Ulysses joined him. "With posters we might get two hundred kids. Maybe even three hundred. Wow! We could make two hundred dollars or more. That's *better* than stealin'."

"I got some great new sides I can bring," Frank said, and began dancing with bent knees and jerking limbs while singing, "Funky David, better take yourself aw-a-ay . . ."

David, resenting the slur, went into a crouch and started looking for an opening to hit Frank. They boxed in a slowly revolving circle for several minutes while the others cheered. Then they went into an embrace-like clinch, patted one another on the back, laughed, and separated. Everyone's tension was lessened by their harmless play. Apparently a play fight was just as good as a real fight to make you feel relaxed and lighthearted afterward.

Fess noticed the change in his gang's mood and saw that the others were following suit. "All right," he said, "go on and listen to her if you want. But I'm warning you, you're letting yourselves in for a lot of trouble. When it starts, and you need a real leader again, you know where to find me." And, rather than admit that he had already lost leadership of the group, he stalked out.

Louretta was glad to see him go, even though she regretted that he had not heard his poem sung. Perhaps—who could say?—it would have put him in a better mood. But she would never know, and the others hardly seemed to miss him.

Jethro, who had been scribbling with a pencil stub in a dirty notebook, looked up.

"Dig," he said. "This is what we gonna put on the poster." And he read aloud:

> The Hawks Take Flight!
> Boss Dance of the Season
> Hawks' Social Club
> 1343 Lambert Avenue
> Admission: Three Eagles

"Now, don't tell me that isn't great—'cause I know it is! All I need's the date!" he rhymed exuberantly.

"If Calvin were only here," Louretta said sadly, "he could draw it for us." She could picture the poster: a huge black hawk flying above bright red letters.

As if in answer to her wish, the door opened, and a smiling, sweatered figure walked in. The gang cheered, and two of the boys rushed over to pound him on the back and ask, "What happened, man?"

"Nothin'," was Calvin's brief comment. "That teacher came for me, and they let me go, that's all."

But before Louretta could ask him to do the poster, his eyes moved swiftly around the room, halted on her at the piano, surrounded by Hawks, and turned dark with anger. Wearing his scowl again, he left as suddenly as he had come. Louretta despaired of ever understanding Calvin. True, artists were supposed to be temperamental, but his lightning changes of mood were very hard to figure out.

The others didn't concern themselves about Calvin, though. They were too involved with their plans for the dance.

"Let's have it before Thanksgiving," Sharon suggested,

probably because she expected her baby in December. It would be her last fling.

"Yeah," Ulysses said practically, "because we don't know if this building has heat or not."

"On a Saturday night," said another boy.

"No, a Friday," said a girl.

They argued about it for several minutes, then finally agreed on Saturday, November tenth.

"That gives us four weeks to get ready. Plenty of time," Ulysses said.

"Oh, it'll be a big success!" Florence exclaimed. "Everybody will come."

"If your brother lets us have it," David said to Louretta.

"And if the Avengers and the cops don't show up," Frank added gloomily.

They *would* have to say those things, Louretta thought.

EIGHT

"I DON'T LIKE IT, LOU," WILLIAM SAID. IT WAS THE TENTH time he'd said it in as many days. "That gang of yours draws the police. If they get rowdy at the dance, the cops will come and close up my shop. Then where will I be? Worse off than I was before, with no business and no more savings, either."

"But William," Louretta protested, "we've already sold tickets and told people."

"And maybe no job either," he went on as if he hadn't heard her. "I've been working so late at the shop, I don't get enough sleep. I've been late twice this week, and the boss caught me napping again today. He didn't like it." He looked at her with red-rimmed, worried eyes. "I shouldn't've listened to you. I should have put those kids out in the first place, the very first day that cop came around. He's been back two more times, and he isn't friendly." William's expression showed utter disgust. "He wants money, of course. They all want money. If you pay off, they leave you alone. But I can't pay, so I'll have to be careful not to break any laws."

With a quick nervous bang of his fist on the table he concluded, "Tomorrow. I'm declaring the place off limits to juveniles tomorrow."

The remains of the cheap but delicious meal—chicken wings, rice and okra—had not yet been cleared from the kitchen table. Momma had gone upstairs to put Cora Lee and Randolph to bed, and the rest of the family had migrated as usual to the front room and the TV set. The chipped white kitchen chairs, their seats still warm, were askew, and chicken bones and grains of rice were scattered at every place. At one end of the table, Louretta and William huddled, whispering to avoid alerting Momma.

That time, though, William had forgotten to whisper.

Louretta forgot too. "You can't do that, William!"

"I'm sorry, Lou, but that's the way it's got to be. I've decided."

"Listen, William," Louretta said, her voice hoarse with urgency, "you can't do that now. You could have done it before, but you can't now."

"Before what?"

"Before I talked them into having the dance."

He stared at her as if she were his worst enemy. "*You* talked them into it? After the cops had just been there complaining about noise? For God's sake, Lou, *why?*"

She put a finger to her lips. "Shhh. Because they were going to do something worse. I didn't want to tell you about it, but now I have to. The boys needed money to buy instruments. They wanted to hold up a store to get it. I talked them into giving a dance instead."

William looked grim. "I knew they were a no-good

bunch of gangsters. I knew it all along. That settles it, Lou. I'm going to padlock that place tomorrow. And you stay away from those kids after this."

"William, *listen*. I told them, if they started that gangster stuff again, they couldn't use the clubhouse any more. So they agreed to have the dance instead. You can't take their meeting place away from them now. Don't you see? It'll mean being good isn't any use. It'll mean nobody believes in them."

William gave her an odd, questioning look. "Why do *you* believe in them so much?"

She was silent for a moment, then said quietly, "Because I have to. There isn't anybody else."

William shook his head disgustedly. His eyes focused on her at last, and they were full of concern. "Listen, Lou, I know I got too much on my mind these days to pay much attention to you. Maybe it would've been different if Poppa had stayed with us. I don't know. The thing is"—he reached awkwardly for her hand—"nobody's ever taken the time to explain things to you. You've never been out of this neighborhood. You don't know the rest of the world isn't like this. But you'll find out someday, if you'll just have a little patience. There are other places and other people. Better people to have for friends. And if you wait just a little while, you'll find them. You've got the stuff in you to go anyplace and do anything you want. Don't ruin your life hanging around with a bunch of bums."

She started to speak in defense of her friends, but William put his finger to her lips.

"No, be quiet and listen to me, Lou. This is important. You let me do what I have to do, so I can make a success of my business, and I'll use the first profits to put you through school. Business school—or even college, if you want. Then my baby sister will have a chance to get away from this place, make a good life for herself, have some *worthwhile* friends."

Louretta was silent. This was what she had always wanted to hear from William. It had always hurt to know he felt her brothers must come first. Now he was showing that he cared just as much about her.

"Is it a deal?"

It was tempting. She thought about it a moment more. Then she said firmly, "No deal. William, if you put those kids out of the building now, they'll go right back to their other plan and steal the money, and then go on to worse things. Can't you see that's just what Lafferty wants them to do? He keeps daring them to do something wrong, so he can have an excuse to arrest them. And if you put them out now, he'll get it."

William was clearly astonished. "You mean, for the sake of that bunch of no-good hoodlums, you'd turn down an offer to send you to college?"

Louretta smiled. "Oh," she said, "you're going to do that anyway."

William laughed ruefully; he knew when he was licked. He had committed himself, and could not back down. He had revealed too much love for her, both to her and himself. "You drive a hard bargain, Sis."

"Tell you what," she said, anxious to compromise. "You can invite some grown-ups to the dance if you want, to make sure the kids behave."

"I'd like to have the whole U.S. Army there," William

declared fervently. "Kids, my foot. Most of them are as big as I am."

"Well, invite an army if you want," she said, then amended it quickly. "I mean four or five. After all, William, it's only a dance."

They had become so absorbed in their conversation that they forgot to lower their voices. Neither of them heard Momma come padding into the kitchen in her stocking feet.

"What dance?" she demanded. "You're too young, Louretta. I don't want you going to dances yet."

Louretta, suddenly inspired, asked, "Even if you're there?"

"What would *I* be doing at a dance?" Momma asked irritably. With the edge of her hand, she began sweeping the leftovers from the table into a dustpan.

"Having fun, maybe," said Arneatha from the doorway against which she leaned, striking as a magazine cover in her flowered rayon pajamas. "You're the best dancer in the family. Any of that sweet potato pie left?"

"I keep too busy cooking for all of you to be thinking about dancing," Momma said. She set down her dustpan and went to the breadbox to get Arneatha a large slice of her delicious homemade sweet potato pie, flavored with lemon and spices. "Here," she said. "Eat it now, before those hungry boys remember there's some left."

Louretta watched with narrowed eyes. Momma's sternness toward Arneatha had only lasted two days. After that, she had relented and gone back to indulging her oldest daughter in her lazy, selfish ways. *Just because she's beautiful*, Louretta thought, though she did not really know why Arneatha deserved such favoritism. Momma was strict with her other children. But Arneatha still went to work when she felt like it, which was seldom, and Cora Lee still didn't know who her mother was. Posing elegantly in her pajamas, long lashes fluttering over her great, velvety black eyes, Arneatha might be a model or a movie star. Except that you seldom saw models and movie stars greedily gobbling sweet potato pie.

"Keep it up," Louretta said sourly. "You'll have a shape like a hippopotamus." But her barb had no sting; Arneatha ate whatever she wanted and remained slim. Pie, ice cream, even having Cora Lee could not harm her gorgeous figure.

"Better that than a face like a pug dog," was Arneatha's cruel answer.

"I wish you children would stop fighting," Momma grumbled, "and try to show some Christian charity in this house. Then maybe I could have some peace once in a while."

"Momma," Louretta pleaded, "*please* listen. The kids are going to have a dance next Saturday night at William's, to raise some money for club activities. We need some grown-ups there to make sure things don't get out of hand. I want *you* to be there, Momma. Please say you'll come."

"And be a chaperone for a bunch of little monsters. *Ugh*," Arneatha said, and made a face as if her pie had turned bitter.

"You must be out of your mind, Louretta," Momma said. "Me at a dance on a Saturday night? Who would look after all these children?"

Louretta shot a significant glance at her older sister,

but Arneatha had chosen that moment to disappear, gliding out noiselessly in her gilded slippers. Louretta sighed, accepting defeat. "Will you ask some of your friends to come, then?"

"Maybe. I'll see," Momma said, meaning that she would forget all about it, and went back to clearing the table. "Right now I got more important things to worry about. Jerutha Jackson is coming by tonight with the coin gleaners she collected for the Ladies' Aid Fund. We have to count up all the money so we can report it in church tomorrow. Now you clear out of here and let me get this kitchen cleaned up before she gets here. That woman cleans like dirt is the devil, and I don't want her talking about me behind my back."

Smiling a little, because nobody could possibly find fault with Momma's housekeeping, but feeling defeated, Louretta went into the stuffy little living room. There were no lights in there except the blue glare that came from the television screen. Stumbling over an obstacle, she muttered crossly, "Move out of the way!" and sat down on the floor, only to find herself also sitting on Gordon's foot and Clarice's elbow.

"Ow!" they both howled simultaneously.

"Well, move then," Louretta retorted. "What makes you think you own all the space around here?"

They grumbled, but rearranged themselves to make room. At any other time this would have been the start of a loud, lengthy argument, but Louretta's brothers and sisters did not want to miss any of the show. It concerned a teenage girl whose problem was that she was being pursued by two boys, though she preferred a third who seemed indifferent to her. She had invited them all to a Hallowe'en party and did not want to offend any of them. Her understanding parents suggested that she solve her problem by turning it into a masquerade party and changing masks throughout the evening to keep the boys confused. She did, with amusing results. The party was held in the family's recreation room, which was as beautiful as a palace and almost as vast, and the girl and her friends were all healthy, handsome, well-dressed and well-behaved. At the end of the evening, amid hilarious laughter, everyone unmasked, and the two unwanted boys good-humoredly kissed their hostess on the cheek and departed contentedly with two other girls, leaving her alone with the third boy who had interested her all along. End of problem.

Louretta sighed. Some people seemed to be so well off that even their *problems* would be blessings to other people. She seldom watched TV because it made her mad to see all those rich, safe, happy people and think about the difference between their lives and hers. Arneatha, she was sure, kept from getting angry by believing that if she used enough makeup and read enough magazines she would become exactly like the TV people, and the younger children did not even notice that there was any difference; from watching the television girls and boys visit Disneyland and ride their private ponies, they got up calmly and went to play with their few broken toys.

But television upset Louretta, and she was glad when someone rapped on the front door and gave her an excuse to turn away from the set.

Little Mrs. Jerutha Jackson resembled her son, Jethro, or vice versa; she had a sharp chin, pointed features, and small merry eyes under an astonishing hat that resembled a basket of cherries. She was a devoted churchwoman, attending services twice a week with Louretta's mother, but she lacked the grim manner Louretta associated with most church people. Church people always had their lips pursed to say "No," because they believed that pleasure was sinful. But Mrs. Jackson seemed to feel that after she had done her duty by the Lord, the rest of the time was hers to enjoy. Louretta was glad to see her.

"My, if you aren't getting to be a big young'un," the little woman exclaimed. "Growin' up handsome, too. Bet all the boys are after you."

Louretta mumbled oh no, it wasn't so, not at all, whereupon Mrs. Jackson smacked her playfully. "Well, if they aren't now, they soon will be. Nothing wrong with it, child. Better enjoy yourself while you can." She sailed toward the kitchen, needing no guide to find her way in the dark. She had been here a hundred times and knew the house perfectly.

Louretta followed, not wanting to let the cheerful little woman out of sight. People like Mrs. Jackson were what she had instead of trips to Disneyland and palace-style playrooms, and she meant to enjoy them all she could.

Momma looked up from her Bible when they entered. "Evening, Jerutha," she said gloomily. "I been trying to find some consolation for only collecting four measly dollars. The Good Book says the Lord loveth a cheerful giver, but I guess the people I asked never heard that verse."

"I 'spect the Lord loves a cheerful *taker*, too," Mrs. Jackson said, " 'cause I made out fine. What I do, I don't ask folks straight out to give to the church. First I jollies 'em up a bit, inquires about their health and generally stands around and passes the time of day. Then when I get around to asking for a contribution, they's right generous."

"How much did you get?"

"Twenty-eight dollars and forty cents," Mrs. Jackson said, and dropped her heavy bundle of coin cases on the table. "That'll buy a lot of supplies for Bible school. Praise the Lord."

"Amen."

"But don't you fret, Rosetta Hawkins. Just try it my way next time. Take it easy, don't try so hard, and you'll do much better. Just like I'm always tellin' you about this old house and these children. Leave 'em be once in a while and enjoy yourself. They'll be better for it, and so will you."

Louretta saw an opportunity. "Don't you think Momma deserves a Saturday night out, Mrs. Jackson?"

"Why, sure, child," Mrs. Jackson said. "That's what I've just been tellin' her. All work and no play makes the soup taste flat."

Louretta didn't think that was exactly the way the proverb went, but she didn't want to quibble about it just then. "Well, will you please ask Momma to come to our dance next Saturday night? And you come too, Mrs. Jackson."

Momma looked up wearily from her Bible. "Louretta, if you don't stop pestering me about that dance, you'll be sorry. I told you, I don't have time for that kind of foolishness. I'm already behind with the Lord's work."

"Maybe this is the Lord's work too, Rosetta," Mrs.

Jackson rebuked gently. "Let's hear what these youngsters are up to."

"Well," Louretta began, "you know we have a music group that meets at my brother's building."

Mrs. Jackson nodded. "Yes, and it's been a fine thing for Jethro. That boy was always so *restless*. But lately he seems to have calmed down some, now he has that place to go to."

"We have a piano and a music teacher and everything. We even compose our own songs," Louretta said proudly, then regretted it under her mother's stern gaze. *Pride is the deadliest of the seven deadly sins. Beware of vanity. Ask the Lord to humble you.*

"Well, anyway," she went on quickly, "this teacher said he would teach the boys to play instruments, and we're giving the dance to raise money to buy them. I think it would be good to have some grown-ups at the dance, just to make sure everything goes all right. And I want you both to come."

Louretta paused, then thought of the final remark that would be sure to remove any remaining doubt from Mrs. Jackson's mind. "Jethro wants to learn the trumpet," she said. "I hope he gets one. I think he's very talented."

"Sho he is," Mrs. Jackson said with pride. "Rosetta, you come on and stir yourself and go to that dance with me. These children are trying to do something fine, and we ought to help them."

"How can I leave this house?" Momma demanded indignantly. "It's different with you, your children are grown. But I have five under twelve. And one of them not yet a year old."

118

"What's wrong with that lazy oldest girl of yours?" Mrs. Jackson retorted. "The baby's hers anyway, isn't it?"

Momma gave a reluctant nod, and lowered her eyes.

"I ain't tryin' to shame you, now, Rosetta. I'm your best friend; you know I wouldn't do that for the world. I'm just statin' what's right. What's happened happened, and nobody's to blame. But you got no cause to be spoilin' that girl so much. Let her keep her hips home one time and look after the children."

Momma was getting desperate for an excuse. "I don't have a thing to wear," she said.

"Patch something together, then," Mrs. Jackson said. "Nobody's going to be looking at two old hens like us anyhow. 'Course I *might* get out on the floor one time and cut me a rug."

Holding her skirt up with one hand, Mrs. Jackson did a few steps that must have been from an ancient dance, though they were not too far removed from the Monkey.

Louretta had a hard time restraining her giggles. Momma was scandalized. "Jerutha Jackson, I thought you'd have sense enough to act your age by now."

"Oh, fooey," Mrs. Jackson said, with a fine, nimble pirouette. "What's age? I like to get out and be around young people. They make *me* feel young. They'd do you good, too. You've been cooped up in this house too long."

"Well," Momma said uncertainly.

Louretta clapped her hands delightedly.

"I haven't said yes yet," Momma said with an angry glance at Louretta.

But Mrs. Jackson was already making plans. "What we'll do," she said, "is sell some refreshments to help these children get the money they need. I'll make a mess of fried chicken, and potato salad, just like I always do for the church suppers. You won't have to cook a thing, Rosetta. Since you're much too old for dancing, you can just sit behind a table all night and sell food."

Momma stood up with an indignant sparkle in her eyes. She looked thirty-five at the most.

"I can dance you into a corner any day," she told Mrs. Jackson. "What's more, I can prove it. Louretta, where are those new records William brought home the other day? You know the ones I mean—the real jumpy ones, 'Shooby Doo' and 'Looby Lou,' whatever they're called."

"I'll get them!" Louretta cried, and ran to the front room, eager to turn off the machine that brought upsetting strangers into the house and turn on the one that would make it happy again.

NINE

LOURETTA SHOULD HAVE KNOWN EVERYTHING WAS GOING
much too well that Saturday. The first floor of the building
was beautifully decorated with crepe paper streamers and
soft colored lights that hid the cracks in the old walls, and
she herself had a curly new hairdo that was worth every
minute of the uncomfortable night she'd spent trying to
sleep on rollers, and a new apple-green dress that William
had paid for.

He'd taken her downtown on a surprise shopping trip
that morning, and they hadn't gone to the second-hand
Thrift Store either. Nor had they gone to one of the cheap
stores where the salesladies glared at you suspiciously and
yelled at you to hurry up, and the gaudy clothes you
bought under this pressure always fell apart the first time
you wore them. No, they'd gone right straight into one of
the big shiny department stores, which was already glit-
tered up for Christmas, and a saleslady had said softly, "May
I help you, Miss?"

Louretta had never been in such a fine store or had a
saleslady speak to her so politely before. On the Avenue,
and in the cheap stores everywhere where poor people

shopped, the merchants screamed at their customers and treated them like criminals or children. Louretta wondered whether a saleslady had ever said, "May I help you, Ma'am?" to Momma in her entire life, and felt sure that the answer was no. Maybe if that had happened, even once, Momma would be different.

Briefly Louretta wished it were her mother who was downtown picking out a dress today. But she changed her mind when the saleslady brought out armfuls of size 8 dresses—pink and orange and navy and red and green, silk and velvet and wool, plain and with collars, pleated and with bows. She tried them all on. Each one was lovelier than the last, making it impossible to decide until William said, "That green one. The pleats will spin out when you dance."

And dance she had, more than ever before in her life, with more boys than she had ever imagined would ever notice her. First with Jethro, who loved to do the Pony because his partner always tired before he did (but Louretta was able to keep up with him); then with Ulysses, who was surprisingly graceful and light on his feet, in spite of his bulk; then with William, whose limp was more noticeable than usual tonight. He must have been worrying a lot lately. Worry and tension always accentuated his limp. But Louretta was much too happy this evening to think about William's worries for long. She resented wasting a dance on her brother because it was obvious that Mrs. Jackson's prediction had come true: Tonight all the boys were after her. Later she might be ashamed of her selfishness, but right now her mind was pleasurably occupied with the large happy crowd, the good music, and her dizzying succession of dancing partners.

A sweet record with a rhythm like a slowed heartbeat began to play, and long, gangling David appeared to ask her to dance. Once again she was annoyed; maybe she had imagined it, but she thought she had seen Calvin starting to move in her direction from a far corner. She'd only had a chance to talk to him once since the day Mr. Lucitanno had arranged his release from the police station. That time, at school, she'd asked him to letter the posters for the dance. Though once he would have been full of enthusiasm for such a project, he declined, and he had not come near the building since. She wanted to tell him how glad she was to see him tonight.

But it was too late; David had reached her first. Far up above her head, his chin bobbed up and down in rhythm to the music as he chewed his gum. Limp and resigned, she let him steer her mechanically around the floor—step left, drag right, step left, drag right—while she stared at the bottom of his tie. David danced awkwardly and off-beat, but the accurate rhythm of his jaw never faltered— up-down, up-down it went, like a metronome. She was on the verge of a giggle when he turned her around suddenly, and she saw Fess.

He had come in, but not very far, and stood, arms folded, with his back to the door, as if on guard. Everything about him—his sad-eyed expression, his awkward wide-legged stance, his sloppy sweatshirt—proclaimed that he had not come to take part in the dancing. No, Fess had something more serious on his mind, and whatever it was cast the first shadow on the bright beginning of her evening.

Then David turned her again, and she brushed against the hard object that bulged in his breast pocket.

"What have you got in your pocket?" she whispered.

Instead of answering directly, he gave her a grim warning. "Listen, baby, if anything happens tonight, hit the floor right away. Don't try to run or you might get hurt. Tell the other girls."

She couldn't believe what she had just heard. "What do you mean? What could happen?"

"A little shooting, maybe," he said casually, without missing a beat with his chewing gum.

Louretta stopped dancing and stepped back. David was so very tall that she had to bend her head far back to look up into his face, and when she did, she saw that it was not babyish any more. It had grown taut and lean, and the eyes that looked down at her from that great height were cool and serious. Maybe he was fourteen now, instead of thirteen. He looked twenty.

Nevertheless she scolded him as if he were still a child. "David, you ought to be ashamed of yourself, talking that way. You're just trying to scare me, and I don't think it's one bit funny. There isn't going to be any shooting around here unless you start it, and I won't let you. Now you take that thing home before I call my brother and have him throw you out."

She started across the floor toward William, but David's ungentle hand on her elbow pulled her back before she could take two steps. His fingers tightened until they hurt her.

"*Ow*, David," she whimpered.

"I'm sorry, Lou, but you was about to blow the whistle on me, and I couldn't let you do that. This is serious. Didn't you see all those cop cars parked around this place when you came?"

Louretta tried to remember, but she really hadn't noticed anything unusual on the Avenue. She probably would not have noticed an entire army, she was so excited about her new dress and the good time she was going to have wearing it. She resented David very much for spoiling that good time.

"In the side streets," he explained, hissing. "They always park in the side streets when they gonna pull off a raid."

"Ohhh," she wailed. "William's right. You're nothing but a bunch of hoodlums. I've been wasting my time with you."

"Sticks and stones," David said coolly. "Call me names if you want, Lou, but that won't change the facts. The word is out that the Avengers are coming down here to waste us tonight. And after they show, the cops will bust in and finish the job. But we gonna be ready for them." He grinned and patted his pocket.

Louretta had already decided she was not going to believe any of this. "You know what I think? I think you boys are making it all up, just so you can have an excuse to fight. You can't be happy just dancing and being nice and having a good time. No, you have to *fight*. There's only one name for people like you. Hood—"

David interrupted her by placing a rough hand over

her mouth. Then he dropped it to her shoulder and said, "C'mon, baby. Let's dance. People are looking at us."

She was too shocked to refuse, but his smile was not a nice one, his embrace was stiff and unfriendly, and as they danced he said, "It's just like Fess always says. Our women are all mixed up."

"Oh, you and your Fess!" she shot back at him. "That mean ugly boy has the rest of you hypnotized. Otherwise you'd see what a nasty little dictator he is."

"Fess says," he went on as if he had not heard her, "our women always side with the white man, and blame *us* for the conditions *he* causes. If somebody attacks us and we fight back, you call *us* hoodlums. Man, you colored women sure have some tricked-up minds."

"Then I certainly won't force you to dance with me," she said, and wrenched herself away from David. But just then the record ended anyhow, making her action pointless.

"Nothin' wrong with you from the neck down, though," David said with an appreciative whistle as she walked away.

That made her angrier than all the rest. The nerve of him, being so fresh! He was only thirteen, after all. A fresh kid trying to act like he was grown was more insulting, somehow, than a full-grown man.

But was David the only one? She looked around at the couples doing the Jerk with frantic shoulder spasms and knees and rears working like pistons. It was more than a dance; it was a pantomime of something else. How many of them would slip off to hallways and alleys later to do the real thing? And how many of them were, like David, carrying concealed weapons, man-sized knives and guns? These things were supposed to be For Adults Only. But not here, not in Louretta's world.

She did not know how to cope with the sudden rush of serious thoughts that did not go with the gaiety around her, so she headed instinctively for the corner table behind which Momma stood serving refreshments. Louretta stood near the table, drawing comfort from her mother's presence, but did not venture to tell Momma what was on her mind. Bustling about, chattering gaily with Mrs. Jackson —who was dressed up, tonight, in an old fur neckpiece and a crown of brown feathers—Momma looked happy and young, younger than Louretta felt right now. Blind Eddie was behind the table too, feasting on chicken and potato salad and joking with the women. He was being treated like a king, and Momma seemed to enjoy spoiling him. Let her have fun for a while; from now on, Louretta would be on her own.

It was terrifying to realize how much she had always depended on Momma at the same time that she knew Momma could no longer really help her.

William, she thought with a flood of relief; William will know what to do. He was old enough to know, yet young enough to listen to her. That had been a silly, spoiled little girl who had resented William's presence at the dance twenty minutes ago; now Louretta was very grateful for her big brother. She started toward the door where he stood, collecting tickets and money and firmly turning away free-loaders. But the floor was crowded with couples doing the Shing-a-Ling, two steps to each side, which took up a lot of room, and before she could get to William the door was flung open, catching him off balance on his weak leg. He toppled, and as he was struggling to get to his feet again, the room suddenly filled with police.

A scream stopped halfway in Louretta's throat and died there. Perhaps because she had half expected the events that followed, she found herself observing them with calm detachment, as if she were not really present, and were only watching them on a TV screen.

Momma, with plates of potato salad in both hands, dropping them both and screaming in Louretta's place, "Lord have mercy!"

William, getting slowly and painfully to his feet, the look of surprise on his face slowly changing to grim resignation.

David, somehow crossing the room in two seconds to arrive at the piano where it was pushed against the wall, and Fess moving sidewise through the crowd to join him and Frank, who was there before either of them. There was something about their swift convergence in that one spot that made Louretta expect trouble.

At least half a dozen couples were still briskly going through the motions of the Shing-a-Ling, but the rest had frozen in their tracks, hands raised to clap, toes pointed out, mouths open, eyes staring. Long after the last couple had stopped dancing, the hit record boomed on senselessly:

> Put your money where your mouth is,
> Or just stop talkin' to me.
> I'm tired of all your big talk,
> I want security . . .

The men in blue moved swiftly among the couples, patting the boys at chest, waist and thigh, and the Man—all two hundred and fifty pounds of him—stood in the center of the floor and roared to make himself heard above the music:

"All right, let's have an orderly search! All boys line up against that wall—hands over your heads, march to the wall, face it, and bend from the waist. Ha ha, that's right." He laughed, for several boys, used to police searches, had assumed the position automatically. "Women and girls over on that wall," he added, motioning with the butt end of his gun. "Get moving!"

Louretta took two obedient steps with the rest of the girls, then halted as she saw William being shoved, like the other males, toward the opposite wall. He refused to go—he was arguing with the officer who had him by the shoulder—and when the officer struck him, Louretta's anger flared up and she became involved with the scene around her. She would never let those crude, clammy-handed cops search her—no, never. She would die first.

But apparently they were only interested in searching the boys. The record had finally ended, and while the amplified needle scratched in the groove, Lafferty's voice rang out clearly.

"Don't waste time. We know they're armed. Get those weapons!"

At least half the boys had moved obediently to the wall, hands over their heads, as Lafferty had directed, but others were resisting, and at their leader's urging, the cops became rough with them. Ulysses, who always moved slowly, was kicked in the back of the knees by a big policeman, and for a moment Louretta feared he was going to strike back. But, after giving the cop a murderous look, he went to the wall. Calvin, who tried to argue with another cop, was grabbed by the shoulder and slammed against the wall so hard Louretta could feel the pain.

"Line 'em up there! Let's get it over with!" Lafferty commanded.

An impulse came to Louretta then that frightened her. What had seemed at first like an army of cops turned out to be only six, including Lafferty, and two of them were as skinny as David and almost as young. The forty or so boys in the room included some who were big and strong, like Ulysses, and others who were armed, like David. If they rushed the cops, they could easily trample and destroy them. Oh, if they only would! *Kill them*, she said behind her teeth, and then, out loud, "*Kill* them!"

As soon as she heard herself say those words, she became frightened. They didn't sound like her.

But no one heard her, and thirty seconds later she had had all she could ever want of fighting and killing.

The tall, young blond cop who had slammed Calvin into the wall turned to find Jethro also lagging behind. Jethro was not moving in the direction of the wall, but he was not exactly standing still, either; he was dancing on his toes, shifting from foot to foot, hopping in place like a crazy marionette.

Please, Jethro, snap out of it, Louretta prayed silently. His behavior looked like a kind of defiance, but she knew he always acted like that when he was nervous and excited.

130

But the cop did not know that, and to make matters worse, *he* was nervous too. He was one of the young ones, tall but not filled out yet, with smooth cheeks below his large pink ears. This might even be his first assignment.

"Get movin' there, fella," he said, not unkindly. "I don't want to hurt you."

But Jethro was unable to move—at least not in the way the officer demanded. In a convulsion of excitement, he continued jiggling in place, while his tongue licked his lips and his eyes darted around the room.

All the other boys, the protesting as well as the obedient ones, were now lined up against the wall in the humiliating search position, and the other policemen were briskly going down the line, patting them. Only Jethro and the young cop remained in the center of the room.

Then Lafferty yelled, "What's holding things up down there?"

Hearing his chief rebuke him, the young cop nervously drew his revolver.

Jethro's legs still did not move forward, only up and down; but he responded. His arms, which had been above his head, came down to his sides.

Lafferty called, "Watch it! He's armed!"

There was a short, deafening explosion, and Jethro yelped, bent double, and dropped to his knees, then rolled over on his back on the floor. The young cop stood over him, looking down with an astonished stare as if he could not believe his pistol had really harmed someone.

With a shriek like a wounded bird, a small bundle of fur and feathers shot out of the corner and collapsed on the floor beside Jethro. The hat had slipped to an even sillier angle, but Mrs. Jackson's face, when she looked up, was grim.

"My boy was nervous. He had epileptic fits. Couldn't you see that? Oh, the Lord will judge you if you've killed him!" She seemed calm, but then her voice rose in that eerie wailing sound again.

Lafferty was bending over Jethro too. "He's not dead," he told Mrs. Jackson shortly, and straightened up. "Curtis, you go call for the rescue wagon."

Glad of an excuse to leave, the young blond cop loped out eagerly. When he had gone, an angry murmur started on both sides of the room and rose to a howl that was like the cry of a single animal. Boys and girls surged forward in one movement, like the stampede of a herd. They surrounded the police, beating them with flailing hands and fists, until the cops waved clubs to beat them off.

"Get back!" Officer Lafferty ordered, drawing his gun. "Any of you try anything else, you'll get what your friend got."

At the same time Mrs. Jackson rose and said with all the dignity of her strong faith, "No, children. 'Vengeance is *mine*, saith the Lord.' *He* will punish them."

The noise and movement subsided, but no one returned to the walls. They stayed where they were, in the center, watching with old, grim eyes in impassive young faces.

Another wail started up in a far corner of the room, a barely-human sound, which Louretta recognized, after a moment, as her mother's voice. At the same time Mrs. Jackson moved aside and she saw Jethro's pale, twisted face

—strange how white *all* people became when they lost a lot of blood—and the pool of it beside him that was spreading to mix with a puddle of darker red liquid.

"All he had in his pocket was a little old wine bottle," Mrs. Jackson said.

And was he drunk? Louretta wondered. *No,* her experience told her immediately. Jethro's nerves were so high-strung that he could get drunk on excitement alone. He needed no alcohol to paralyze him.

"He could have been going for a weapon, ma'am," Lafferty said, almost apologetically. "The officer had to defend himself."

No one said anything. The silence was worse than an accusation.

Louretta learned then that even the most powerful bullies could squirm. Lafferty began to sweat. He turned to William, as if appealing to the man in charge.

"We were in the right here. We had information that a rumble was scheduled to take place. People might have been killed. We had to search for weapons."

"Did you find any?" William asked softly.

Lafferty reddened. His eyes, which had been almost moist with pleading, hardened like ice cubes. "You saw it," he declared. "You saw this boy make a move toward his pocket, like he was reaching for a weapon."

William stared the officer down with his large soft eyes until Lafferty looked away. "No, Officer, I didn't see anything," he said with almost insulting politeness.

Louretta was so proud she almost cheered for William. Several others did it for her.

Lafferty was bright red now, and sweat was running

down his face. As if he had suddenly remembered his power, his voice changed to a hoarse bellow. "All right —where's your license to hold a public dance?"

William answered in the same soft voice, "You've already seen my license several times, Officer. It's on the wall in the back room."

"That's a license to operate a commercial printing establishment," Lafferty said. "It doesn't entitle you to run a dance hall.

William just stood there, leaning slightly on his good leg as if his weak one pained him, but not showing any other reaction.

"When we got here tonight you were on the door, collecting money?" Lafferty's question was actually a statement.

William nodded, his face expressionless.

"All right then!" the policeman cried triumphantly. "You were operating illegally. We're closing you up. You don't open for business again until you've gone before a judge."

William nodded again.

Lafferty's voice dropped, as if he wanted only William to hear. "And the judge may close you up *permanently*, unless you show more cooperation."

William's lips were pressed tightly together, but the lower one trembled. It was the only sign that he was upset. With a shrug, as if saying, "Is *that* all? That's not so bad," he turned his back on Lafferty and lit a cigarette.

This time Louretta did cheer for William, three spontaneous whoops, and so did several others. But as the irate officer whirled to deal with them, the ambulance crew hurried a stretcher through the door, distracting him and sobering all the boys and girls. They watched somberly as the crew slid Jethro onto the stretcher and carried him out swiftly. Several rough-mannered boys, who normally danced, ate, even slept with their hats on, removed them as the stretcher passed them with its small burden. How little Jethro must weigh, after all. Louretta really hated that rookie cop when she thought about that. No matter how young the cop was, he was a man, with a man's strength, and he did not need to use a gun against a frail fourteen-year-old boy who weighed less than a hundred and twenty pounds. Mrs. Jackson followed the stretcher, and Louretta's mother, her arm around the little woman's waist, went with her.

The ambulance sirens opened up on the Avenue. Yelling, "All right! Let's clear this place," the cops began hustling the girls and boys outside.

"Don't push us, mustard plaster," Joella said to one policeman who was shoving her too hard.

"You're lucky we didn't take you in," he answered.

"Take us in? For what? *You're* the murderers!" was plucky Sharon's reply.

"Murderers!" Joella echoed.

The angry buzzing went through the crowd again, and the cops suddenly became much more polite. They went around courteously and asked the remaining youths to please leave. Louretta knew why their manner had changed. They had been reminded that they were in the wrong, and knew they couldn't afford to make any more enemies. One of them had shot an unarmed boy in front of a hundred witnesses. Unless at least one of those witnesses could be made to say it was in self-defense, they were in trouble.

"Sir, would you and the young lady mind leaving now?" a dark, burly cop asked William. He spoke stiffly, as if the polite words were choking him.

"Yes, we *would* mind," William told him. "This is my place of business. And this is my sister. She and I want to stay and collect a few of our things."

The policeman looked questioningly at his chief.

"Yeah, let 'em get their things out tonight," Lafferty told him gruffly. "They won't be able to in the morning. Give them half an hour. We'll wait outside."

"All right," the dark cop told William. He glanced at the pool of spilled blood and wine on the floor, then looked away quickly. "Just don't touch the, uh, evidence."

"I wouldn't dream of it," William assured him with that same insulting politeness.

The policeman touched his cap nervously and followed Lafferty and the others outside, leaving Louretta and William alone in the building. She looked around at the room that had seemed so gay when she had arrived what seemed like years ago—the dirty, trampled floor with its hideous splotch of color, the discarded paper cups and plates, the torn, discouraged crepe paper streamers that dangled from the ceiling. Then she looked at her brother, who had made such a wonderful show of calmness and strength. He looked tired now, and was trembling.

"William," she said, moving closer to him, "I was so proud of you tonight. They wanted you to help them get away with it, and you wouldn't."

136

For answer he reached out and rubbed her hair.

"But you've lost your business. Oh, *William!*" she wailed.

"You've lost something too, Sis," he said gravely. "A chance to go to college."

College was something she'd never had anyway, something far away that belonged to a different world, so losing it didn't matter.

"Who cares?" she said, almost gaily, though it was not a gay moment. "Let's get our things together so we can get out of here."

"Right," he said.

She thought a minute. "Let's see. Momma's big bowl, and her two platters, and our silverware. And your record machine."

"And my records," he added. "And the menus I printed today. My last job, maybe, but I intend to deliver it on schedule."

"Poor William," she said in commiseration. Then she thought of Jethro. "Oh, it's all so *awful!*"

The tightness of his smile warned her that this was a moment when she dared not cry. The first of many such moments, probably.

He gave her hair another rough pat. "We'll make do, Sister Lou," he said gruffly, and went into the back room.

She hated to be thinking about forks and spoons while Jethro was lying in the hospital, but there was nothing she could do for him now, and her family would have to eat as usual tomorrow. So she moved around the room mechanically, avoiding the bloody patch in the center of the floor, picking up pieces of tableware from the serving table, the floor, the chairs, the piano.

The piano! As she picked up the twelfth spoon, last of the set, from its top, she saw a picture, like a photograph, of Frank and David and Fess all standing there where no one had been five seconds before, and remembered the funny feeling she'd had then, as if something were going on that she didn't understand.

She ran to the back room and said excitedly, "William, come here! Don't say anything, and don't ask me why—I may be crazy—but I want you to look in the back of the piano."

He set his stack of menus down and followed her. Together they managed to slide one end of the heavy piano away from the wall. Then they stared at what was inside the back of it. Nestling among the strings was a whole arsenal of rusty knives and homemade guns.

William made a soundless whistle.

"What are you going to do, William?"

He lit a cigarette and thought a moment. Then he said, "Help me shove this back against the wall, before the cops get suspicious and come back in here."

"There," he said when the piano was back in place. "Now let that be our little secret, Lou."

"I don't understand."

"Can you think of a better hiding place?" he asked with a wink.

He was not going to betray her friends. "Oh, William!" She flung her arms around his waist in a quick, grateful hug.

The horns of the police cars began beeping impatiently, warning them that it was past time to leave. William turned out the lights and locked the door, then handed the keys to the officer who was waiting outside to padlock the building. Louretta carried the dishes and silver and the freshly printed menus, William the records and the record player. They were heavily laden, but they managed to hold themselves tall and keep their heads up proudly, ignoring the patrol cars parked all along the block.

At last they reached the little house and let themselves in. They dumped their burdens on the floor. The house was quiet and dark, as if nothing at all had happened. Their brothers and sisters were all sleeping peacefully. Let them be peaceful for a little while longer, Louretta thought.

William's match was the only light until she found the little lamp in the corner. "William," she whispered, "when we found the guns and knives, I was afraid you would tell the cops. Anything you did would have been all right with me, but I was afraid because of the way you used to say the kids were hoodlums."

"What's that got to do with tonight?" he asked.

"Well, the guns were really there. So that proves you were right, doesn't it? They *are* hoodlums."

"Lou," William said seriously, "I learned something tonight. Those cops can't tell the difference between a respectable Negro and an outlaw. They treated me just as rough as everybody else. So that makes us *all* outlaws, at least in their eyes."

He began to rub his aching shoulder in the spot where

the cop had pushed him, until Louretta took over and rubbed it for him.

"And if they can't tell the difference," he concluded, with a groan as she found the sorest spot, "who am *I* to judge?"

"And if you can't judge," she echoed with a kiss on his cheek, "who am *I?*"

TEN

THE SKY ON THE NEXT TWO MORNINGS MATCHED LOURETTA'S mood—gray and dull and gloomy, so thick it seemed it would never part to show the sun again. All day Sunday Louretta stayed in her room, avoiding the rest of the family. But on Monday morning she had to get dressed and come downstairs. Bernice, Clarice, Gordon and Andrew were all in their places, and Momma was in the kitchen dishing up bowls of hot cereal as if nothing had happened, though she had not been to bed for two nights and still wore the purple rayon crepe dress she had worn to the dance. It had been a pretty dress, but it was stained and wrinkled now, and her eyes were shot through with little red streaks.

When Louretta came in she said, "I tried to make Jerutha Jackson come home with me this morning and rest for a little while. But she won't leave that place."

Louretta took the cereal her mother offered and slid into her chair. She did not look at or touch her food.

"What place, Mom? A bar?" fresh Gordon wanted to know.

"Yeah, Momma, you look like you was out drinkin' all weekend," Andrew chimed in.

"Hush your smart mouths and show some respect," Momma told them, but her remark was half-hearted. On any other day she would have added two back-handed slaps and a Bible quotation without missing a beat of her stirring spoon. Momma did not believe in halfway measures in raising children. When discipline was called for, she gave them a little lecturing, a little discomfort *and* a little religion, knowing at least one would take effect.

Louretta didn't want to bring up the subject of Jethro in front of the children, but she could not restrain herself.

"How is he, Momma?"

Momma sighed.

"Well?"

"They don't know. He might make it, and he might not. He's a mighty strong little fella, though. Doctor told me yesterday, most people wouldn't've lived *this* long."

"Who you talkin' 'bout, Momma?" Bernice asked.

"Say, what happened at the dance?" Andrew asked Louretta. "You haven't said a word about it."

No Sunday newspapers had been bought, either, which brought bitter complaints from the children, who missed the comics. But these days not much could be kept from Andrew. Going on thirteen and getting taller all the time, he was a handsome boy with bright brown eyes that reflected his quick intelligence. Those large, alert eyes were sharply trained on his sister now.

"Nobody," she said, avoiding them. "Nothing happened. Say, aren't you kids late for school?"

"You might as well tell us," Clarice said practically. "We'll find out at school anyway."

"Brats," Louretta said. "Get out of here."

As Andrew passed she reached out suddenly and gave him a quick, fierce hug. He was not such a little boy any more. He was getting to be just about Jethro's size.

"Hey, lemme go!" Andrew cried resentfully, and pulled away. He hated shows of affection. When she released him he ran out of the house as fast as he could.

When they had gone, Momma spoke in her other voice, her talking-to-grown-ups voice. "Louretta, you round up some of them big, strong boys at school today and send them over to the hospital. Jethro needs five pints of blood."

"I wish I could give it all myself," she said. "Then maybe I would die."

"Don't talk like that," her mother said sharply. "You got no call to be blamin' yourself for what happened."

"Why not?" Louretta asked her. "It was my idea to have that dance. I talked the kids into it. I even talked *William* into it."

The light went out of her mother's eyes. "Don't know which is worse," she said, "havin' a son who's dyin' of a bullet wound, or one who's dyin' of a broken heart. I don't mind sayin' I blame you for what's happened to William, Louretta. If you hadn't got him to rent that place he wouldn't have grown so set on having that printing business. Oh, he would have thought about it a while, but eventually he would of forgot it and settled down to his job. Now he's had his big dream and lost it, and that's worse than never havin' it at all."

Yesterday William had been glum and silent, moving around the house like a shadow. Louretta hadn't spoken to him, but apparently Momma had.

"Is it, Momma?" Louretta wondered. "I'm not so sure."

Momma rocked back and forth in her straight chair. "Folks got to learn it's not good for them to think too big and want too much. It's better to be satisfied with what they have."

"When you say 'folks,' you mean *our* folks, don't you?"

"What other kinds of folks you think I mean?" Momma snapped. "I ain't studyin' about no white folks. Never have." She had stopped rocking, and sat straight up in her chair.

"But that's not fair," Louretta said.

"Fair?" Momma said harshly, with infinite scorn. "Whoever told you this world was supposed to be fair?"

Then, as if she remembered Louretta's age and was afraid she had said too much too soon, she began to rock again, and to hum:

> Swing low, sweet chariot,
> Comin' for to carry me home.
> Swing low, sweet chariot . . .

It only emphasized her point. Once you accepted that things were not supposed to be fair in this world, all you could do was hope they would be better in the next. Now Louretta understood why her mother clung so tightly to the church. But the church had never meant that much to Louretta. Yesterday, for instance, she hadn't even thought of going. She had always been too eager to live in this world to worry about the next. Always sure that if she tried hard enough she could make things better *now* for herself and others.

Louretta looked out through gray windows streaming with rain, and was overwhelmed by all the havoc she had caused in trying to do good. Getting William to rent the place. Inviting the kids there. Having that dance. If she had left Jethro in the alley, if she had let him go ahead and steal a few hub caps, he would be well today. How arrogant she had been, making plans for everybody, how sure of herself, and how selfish—thinking only of her social life, never of William. And how terrifyingly wrong.

"Then it's all my fault," she said bleakly. "Everything."

"You couldn't know," Momma said. "Don't fault yourself, child. You couldn't know what would happen."

"I could have asked somebody," she said angrily. "You, maybe."

"Would you have listened to what I said?"

That, spoken in her mother's calm, adult voice, was too much. Louretta folded her arms on the table, and put her head on them, and began to sob. "You always blamed me," she cried unreasonably. "You always blame me for everything." It didn't make sense, she wasn't even sure what it meant, but it was absolutely true at that moment, and more than enough reason to spend the rest of her life crying.

Momma's hand touched her head. "Don't be taking it so hard, child. You're too big to be carrying on like that. Besides, you can't do nothing about what's past. All you can do is pick yourself up and go on from here."

Louretta looked up with streaming eyes. "Go where?" she asked. There was no place on earth she wanted to be except here in her mother's kitchen.

"Well, to school, right now."

"Ugh," Louretta commented, and put her head down again.

"Jethro needs those blood donations."

Louretta sat up, no longer crying. "Then I'll go," she said. "But only today, Momma. They don't teach you the truth in school."

"Well, of course they don't," Momma said serenely. "White folks can't stand the truth. It would show up how ornery they are. But I reckon you better go listen to 'em anyway. They set a lot of store by it."

"'Bye, Momma," Louretta said with a kiss on the warm brown cheek. "Get some rest. I'll stay home tomorrow."

School was a mammoth gray stone building with tall iron gates and round towers at each corner. Once she had compared it to a castle, but today it looked more like a dungeon. Inside they taught you lies like "The policeman is your friend" and "Anyone can grow up to be President in America." It was as bad as the church, another big gray stone building, where they taught you that God is just.

It seemed that the biggest and fanciest buildings were the places where they taught the biggest lies. If it were up to Louretta she would tear them all down and hold classes and services in the open air, to let a little truth in. But since she couldn't, she decided she would never go to church again, and would drop out of school as soon as she was old enough. This morning, as she trudged inside, she was certainly in no mood for poems about hard work and dedication and mottoes about democracy and lec-

146

tures about Liberty and Justice for All. But she had at least a year and a half more of it to endure before she would be sixteen. How could she possibly stand it? When she was dumb enough to believe all the fine-sounding, hopeful words, she had loved school, but now she was impatient to get away. Maybe if she cut enough classes, they would expel her. Louretta turned on her heel and made for the nearest exit.

But Mr. Lucitanno, who was twice her age but still believed in all the mottoes, stood blocking her path with his broad, silly smile.

"Good morning, Louretta."

"Morning," she said sullenly.

"Got a minute? I'd like to talk to you."

Mutely she followed him to the classroom that was assigned as his homeroom, and stood while he settled himself at his desk and fumbled with some papers.

"Have a seat."

"No thank you."

His black eyebrows quivered, but he said, "As you wish. Louretta, I just wanted to tell you I heard about what happened over the weekend, and I'm as sorry as I can be. I just want you to know we're doing everything we can to make amends."

Make amends for Jethro? Louretta's response to that was a short, harsh laugh.

Mr. Lucitanno's eyebrows shot up to his hairline. "People aren't all against you," he said. "You have a lot of friends. A committee of teachers is going to City Hall at noon to see if we can't get things straightened out. We're going to demand an end to police harassment of your group, and ask that the building be reopened immediately."

"What for?" Louretta asked.

The young teacher's eyes crinkled up in pain, exactly like William's. *Good*, she thought.

"Why—so you can carry on with your activities," Mr. Lucitanno said in bewilderment. "We're going to request that the City give you some money, too. That way you can afford to buy recreation equipment and supplies. And maybe you can get a regular staff of teachers and recreation leaders—not just volunteers." His sunny smile had returned. "Who knows, maybe some good will come of all this. It's an ill wind that blows no good, you know."

He beamed his idiotic smile at her.

"We don't want any teachers," Louretta said. "They just teach us a lot of lies and confuse us, anyway. Let the building stay closed. I've decided the clubhouse wasn't such a good idea."

"Oh, no, Louretta!" he cried. "It was a *wonderful* idea!"

"When you don't know what you're doing," she said, trying to teach him what she had learned, "it's better to leave things alone."

"Just because you had a little trouble at the start doesn't mean you should abandon your whole idea."

A little trouble? Louretta laughed again at this. "Sorry, Mr. Lucitanno," she said, "I got to go now."

"What's your hurry?"

"Got to round up some blood donors for Jethro."

"What type of blood does he need?"

Louretta gave him a long, insulting look. "Any type but white."

148

The teacher blushed deeply under his olive skin, but he did not give up. "I'll go to the hospital as soon as I leave school," he said quietly. "You're not doing your friend any favor with your attitude, Louretta. Blood is just blood. It's all red, and if you were as sick as he is, you'd know it. I think Jethro will welcome my blood as much as anyone else's."

"Suit yourself," she said with a shrug, and walked out coolly, leaving Mr. Lucitanno frowning at his desk. If he were a woman, she was sure, he would be crying. It served him right. Why did white people always think they deserved extra gratitude when they offered to help you? Let him get along without it, and see if he would still be so friendly and helpful. She doubted it.

After walking boldly into the principal's office and inquiring, she found Ulysses and Frank and David in the wood shop where they were assigned that period. She was supposed to be in English class, but it could wait. Longfellow and all the rest of those patriotic squares could wait forever, for all she cared. Girls weren't supposed to be allowed in the shop, but she didn't care about that, either.

The three boys jumped at the chance to give blood. They had been fooling around aimlessly all weekend, itching for something to do, and had finally decided on school this morning because there was nothing else.

"Besides," David said eagerly, "this shop is boss. The teacher don't know it, but I'm making me a new gun."

"Yeah," Ulysses said, touching a stone which was supposed to be used for sharpening the shop tools, "and in between working on that bookcase over there, I got me a old knife I'm sharpening so fine it'll slice up bricks."

"Who's the knife for?" Louretta asked.

"Anybody who messes with him, baby," David said, giving Ulysses a significant look.

Ulysses ignored it. "We got one particular party in mind," he said. "The party who tipped the cops off about us."

"Anything I can't stand, it's a pigeon," Frank said. "And if Jethro dies, you better believe there's gonna be a *dead* pigeon on the Avenue."

"They'll have to have a double funeral," David said.

"Or a triple one," Ulysses amended.

"Who do you think it was?" she asked.

The boys glanced at each other, as if asking themselves whether they could trust her. Then Frank laughed. "Hell, she might as well know. What can she do to stop us? We think it was that little punk Calvin."

"He had plenty of time to talk to the cops," Ulysses explained. "He was down at the station a long time, and they probably scared him with what they would do to him if he didn't talk."

"That doesn't prove anything," Louretta said. "Besides, he didn't know anything to tell them, did he? He wasn't a member of the gang."

"He could have heard us talking," David said.

"Don't defend him *too* hard, baby," Frank said with an ugly smile. "The other party we have in mind is your brother."

"*William?*"

"That so-and-so Lafferty used to come around every week and go in the back room and have a conference with William," Frank said. "Now, you tell *me* what they were talkin' about all the time back there? In my book, anybody who talks to a cop that much is a pigeon."

"He don't belong to the gang either," David said significantly. "But he has ears."

"You're wrong about William," Louretta said. "You're as wrong as you can be. If it weren't for him, you'd all be in jail right now."

They stared at her. "What do you mean?" asked David.

She lowered her voice, because the shop teacher was approaching. "I mean he and I found where you had put your guns and things, after the dance was over and the cops and everybody else had gone. And William pushed the piano right back against the wall and didn't say a word to anybody."

They were silent for a minute, taking this in. Silent, and ashamed.

Then David apologized, "Gee, sorry, baby."

"Our mistake," Frank said.

"But don't you see—" she pleaded, "you could be just as wrong about Calvin, too? Promise me you won't do anything until you get some real proof."

Frank, who was the leader when Fess wasn't around, hesitated. Then he said, "We won't do anything now, Lou. But the Hawks don't play around. When we at war, we at war. I can't promise you *what* we'll do if Jethro don't make it."

"Then, for God's sake," Louretta urged, "get yourselves over to that hospital."

ELEVEN

LOURETTA NEVER WENT TO HER ENGLISH CLASS THAT DAY—
nor to any of her other classes, for that matter. As she went
down the hall past Miss Hodges' room, she thought she
heard a clear, musical voice calling her name. It sounded
very much like the little teacher's, but Louretta did not
look back. She kept moving, down the hall, out the side
exit, off the school grounds.

There was nothing in school for her that day, now
that she had learned that all the poems and stories about
goodness and justice were lies. Oh, they were true for some
people, the ones like Mr. Lucitanno, but not for those on
the outside.

The Outsiders. Once you looked, you saw there were
plenty of them everywhere. Take the just-past-school-
age group lounging on the sidewalk outside the school
building—Sharon, who had finally quit to have her baby,
and ragged Roger, who had dropped out a year or so ago,
and the older, unemployed group with whom they min-
gled—all shabby, thin, sullen, with hard eyes and a scorn-
ful way of talking. And aimless, restless feet that had no-
where to go.

Louretta had always wondered why these people, so near her age, did not accept her as one of them. Now she knew. She had had faith and hope, and they had lost those things long ago. They had been Outsiders, and she had not been.

But now hands were raised in greeting as she passed. "Hey." "What's happenin'?"

"Hey," Louretta said in return, and added "Nothing," observing the ritual and being truthful too. Nothing ever happened to Outsiders. She hurried on, for today she had something to do, someplace to go. But tomorrow, or the next day, she would probably join one of the corner groups.

She walked the twelve blocks to the hospital because she did not have carfare, shivering in her poplin coat with its thin wool lining. But the cold outside was not nearly as bad as the deep new chill she felt in her heart.

Once you became an Outsider, everyone knew. After a brief glance, the woman behind the information desk at the hospital spoke to Louretta as if she were not really there, and looked at her without seeing her.

"I'm sorry, but the Jackson boy is not allowed any visitors except members of the immediate family. Are you a member of the immediate family?"

Outsiders did not hesitate to lie to squares; they felt obligated to be truthful only to one another. "Yes," Louretta said.

"Then you may go up," the woman said, still not looking at Louretta. "He's in Room 8-B."

Louretta started for the elevator, but the woman called her back.

"Just a minute. The Jackson boy is on the critical list. No visitors under sixteen allowed."

Louretta wondered for a moment whether she could lie about her age and get away with it. But the woman's pale, suspicious eyes were really taking her in now, ankle socks, braids and all.

"What is your relationship to the Jackson boy?"

"His name is Jethro!" Louretta shouted, tired of hearing him called by that impersonal label. It sounded, she thought, as if he were already dead. Or might as well be.

"Yes," the woman said, unaffected.

Louretta became numb again. It was much better not to have feelings if you were an Outsider, or you would go around hurt and angry all the time. Play it cool was the rule.

"Never mind," she said. "Can you tell me where you go to give blood?"

The woman lapsed back into her bored, automatic voice. "Ground floor, Room G-10," she recited. "Take the elevator down and turn to your right."

Louretta considered sneaking up to Jethro's room anyway. It would be simple, now that she knew his room number, to go up in the elevator instead of down. And the nurses and doctors would probably be too busy to notice her. But then she decided that if the hospital did not want him to have visitors, it was probably because he was not well enough yet.

She pressed the "G" button, went down alone, and got out in a long, dark tunnel. It was the hospital's service floor. She passed storerooms full of mops and brooms and linen, a huge kitchen where everything seemed to be made of gleaming stainless steel, a vast, steaming laundry. All the workers who toiled in this long, dark tunnel seemed to be black and dressed in dingy gray uniforms, just as upstairs, in the brightly lit lobby, everyone was white and dressed in snowy white. As she reached doors marked "X-Ray" and "Hematology," the corridor became lighter, and so did the workers and their uniforms.

"G-10" was marked "Blood Bank" and had a waiting room with long, hard wooden benches. Through an open door she could see a row of hospital beds and nurses passing back and forth wheeling trays of bottles.

"Which patient are you here for?"

The young doctor who asked her this had a sunny, hopeful smile that reminded her of Mr. Lucitanno's.

"Jethro Jackson," she told him without an answering smile.

"Ever give blood before?"

She shook her head.

"Well, then, we'll have to puncture your thumb a little, to find out what type you have. But don't be scared. It won't hurt."

"I'm not," she said, and held out her hand.

"Name? Address? Age? Ever had TB? Syphilis?"

She answered the first four questions while he wrote down the answers on a pad, but at the last, she bristled and said, "I don't think that's any of your business."

"It doesn't matter. It'll show on the blood test anyway." He put the pad away. "That's all. Now let me stick your thumb."

She barely felt the prick of the needle. She watched without emotion as he squeezed a bright red drop of her blood on a piece of glass and took it away.

He came back with a piece of machinery attached to a long rubber tube. "The analysis will take a few minutes, so we might as well get acquainted, Louretta."

She gave him a hard stare; he had sandy hair, freckles, and a likeable smile, but she did not like to have strangers call her by her first name. Especially white strangers. *One thing white people always got to do, no matter how low they are*, Momma always said. *They got to be first-naming you soon as they meet you.*

"Miss Hawkins," she corrected, reading his pin: *Dr. Henry Smith*. "Unless you want me to call you 'Henry.'"

He did not call her anything after that. "Uh—why aren't you in school today?"

Instead of answering she gave a shrug.

"*I* know," he said. "You were so anxious to help your friend, you took off from school and came here. That was very nice of you. I can see you're a very nice girl."

Was he about to get fresh? Louretta looked at him narrowly. But the intern's face was innocent and serious.

"That Jackson boy's a bad case. I was on duty in Emergency when they brought him in. But they're doing all they can for him, and believe me, this is one of the best hospitals in the city. He's getting the best of care. And the police who were involved are paying the entire bill. Did you know that?"

"They ought to be here giving blood, too," she said bitterly.

"I don't understand you kids," the intern said, blushing

—which showed that he understood very well. He took her blood pressure without saying another word. The rubber tube tightened around her arm like a snake as he squeezed the bulb, then relaxed when he let go.

"I'm sorry," he said, very impersonally. "Your blood pressure's a little low. Not enough to worry about, but it's below the limit our regulations require."

She stood up to leave, but he put his hand on her arm.

"No, wait for your blood report. You might as well find out what type blood you have. It's a good thing to know in an emergency. I'll get it for you now."

He hurried off, stopping before he went through the door to call back anxiously. "Wait for me, now."

She shrugged, wondering why it was so important to him. But she stayed.

He was back within two minutes. "You're Type 'O,'" he announced proudly. As if he were responsible for her blood type! "That's very good. It means you can give blood to anyone or take it from anyone." He came closer and lowered his voice. "But your red cell count is a little low. We couldn't have taken blood from you even if your pressure had been up to normal. Ever take iron tablets?"

She shook her head.

"Well, you'd better start. You can buy them at any drug store. Eat lots of liver and spinach, too." He touched her thin sleeve. "And you should wear a warmer coat in this weather."

Except for pulling her arm away, she did not show any reaction to this information. "Can I go now?" she asked.

He reddened so deeply the freckles disappeared.

"Look, girl, I'm trying to help you, don't you understand? This could be serious. You're not anemic, but you're close to it. You're an intelligent girl. Surely you can understand the importance of taking care of yourself."

He was practically shouting at her. His face was tomato-colored.

Louretta let him stand there in silence for a minute after he had finished. Then she asked, very softly, "Mister, you gonna buy those things for me?"

He remained speechless while she stood, looking at him steadily, for another minute.

"I didn't think so," she said finally, and turned to leave. She had taken several steps down the corridor when the intern trotted up behind her and touched her on the shoulder.

She turned in surprise. "Yes?"

"I just wanted to say—you were right about the police. They *should* give blood for your friend."

She did not answer at first; just looked at his face, saw the complexion clearing and the freckles returning as the blush faded. You could tell he felt much better.

"Yes," she said, and offered her hand.

"Well—good-by, Miss Hawkins," he said awkwardly, shaking it. "Take care, now."

"Good-by, Doctor Smith."

Louretta walked along singing to herself for two blocks until she realized what she was doing, and stopped. What on earth did she have to be so happy about? Then she remembered the brief exchange with the intern. She might never see him again in her life, but the last part of their conversation had made her happy.

She reminded herself that losing your "cool" could be fatal. It could lead to all sorts of dangerous habits, like trust and faith and hope. Louretta wanted nothing to do with any of those square feelings again. They led to disappointments which let you down too hard.

As if inviting the air to chill her through and through, she gulped in great frosty lungfuls as she walked into the wind. Thinking about Jethro helped to numb her feelings again. So did the 1300 block of the Avenue, when she reached it and saw the cruising patrol cars and the knot of policemen guarding the building. Lafferty was not among them, but the baby-faced one who had shot Jethro stood in the doorway in an arrogant pose, twirling his club like a drum major in a parade.

"Wouldn't you love to have a .38 to shoot him down?"

The rasping voice coming from the doorway behind her did not surprise her. She was ready for it. She turned toward the ugly face with eyes glittering with cold fire behind the round lenses and an upper lip lifting in a smile that was really a sneer. Frosted air came from his mouth and nostrils like smoke. Time to do what Momma hated most, and make a pact with the Devil.

"I'd sell my soul for one," she said.

Fess laughed gratingly. "Really? I thought you were a strictly non-violent chick. Turn the other cheek, love your oppressors, and all that bull."

"That was before Saturday," she said.

He laughed again. "Jesus didn't do much to help you the other night, did he? Maybe pretty soon you'll get tired of prayin' to your white Jesus. Maybe pretty soon you'll be ready to do something for *yourself*."

159

She shrugged. "Aaah . . . you know."

He caught her meaning immediately. Only an Outsider, someone who no longer believed in anything, could shrug like that and speak with such a weary inflection. "Maybe you *are* ready now. But you sure weren't before. I told the gang what would happen. You remember. I told them, but you wouldn't let them listen to me."

Her eyes shifted across the street. "Those mother-jumping cops," she said bitterly.

His eyes lit up with pleasure. He put a hand on her shoulder. "I believe you *are* ready," he said. "Look, chick —Lucretia or whatever your name is—you're not a bad chick, but you had no business takin' over the leadership from me that day. Women have a place in this movement, but they can't be the leaders. Not in a war."

"What movement? What war?" she wondered aloud.

He gave her a patronizing look. "There's a lot happenin' you don't even know about, baby. There's *so* much you don't understand. But I might give you a chance to learn. You want a chance to learn?"

Thumbs hooked in his leather jacket, he rocked back on his heels in an arrogant pose, waiting for her to beg him. She was conscious of the same old feeling of resentment that always welled up in her whenever she talked to this boy. But what did she have to lose now? "Yes, please," she said.

He wrote down an address and handed it to her. "Come to this address tomorrow night. The meeting starts at eight o'clock sharp. The password is 'Lumumba.' "

"*Password?*" she echoed in surprise. It made her

think of the secret societies little kids had—passwords, codes, secret meeting places.

But he was serious. He nodded his head in the direction of the cops across the street. "We have to be careful." Then he looked her up and down in a new, faintly possessive way that made her uncomfortable. "One of the first things you'll have to do is cut off all that hair."

Her hands flew protectively to her thick, brown, plaited mane. It was as much a part of her as her face or her name.

"Oh, not for tomorrow night," he reassured her. "They'll let you slide for a while. But all our girls wear the African look."

She had seen them striding along the Avenue, first a few, then more and more of them, hair cropped in woolly caps close to their heads, huge earrings swinging like knives. Without the earrings they would have been mistaken for boys. She had wondered about this new fad and why it was growing, without connecting it to any sort of movement, and she had admired the look on some of the girls, the ones with the most purely African features, but had never considered it for herself. She wouldn't like her hair short. But there would be time to think about that.

"Thanks, Fess," she said, and put the paper away carefully. "Listen. I want to ask a favor. Jethro needs blood."

"Um?" he said, pretending not to listen while he stared at something on the distant horizon.

She pulled at his sleeve. "I said, Jethro needs blood. He has four pints but he needs five. I was at the hospital today to give some, but they wouldn't take mine, on account of low blood pressure or something. Would you go and give a pint in my place?"

"Me? No, baby, I ain't got time," he said, and started to edge away.

"I don't understand," she said.

"*I said*, I ain't got time. I have a lot of things to do."

He was moving off. She grabbed his coat sleeve and pulled him back. "Listen, this is important. It could save his life."

He knocked her hand away as if it were an insect. "I don't want to save his life," he said coldly.

As she stared at him in shock, he explained, "Look, if you gonna join the movement you gotta get realistic, baby. And tough, too. You got to be tough. Jethro alive ain't no use to us. But Jethro *dead* can help us wake up this whole town."

And then, because she still stood there with her mouth open, he added roughly, "Look, baby, don't blame me. I didn't shoot him. Blame that cat over there." He jerked his thumb toward the young policeman. "That dumb cop don't know it, but he's done the black people of this city a favor. A great big favor."

He seemed to take pity on her then. He patted her shoulder and said almost kindly, "Come to that meeting tomorrow night. It'll help you understand. See you there."

With a chuck of his fingers on her arm, he was gone around the corner.

Dazed and numb, but grateful for her numbness, Louretta wandered into the alley that led from the Avenue to her street.

She was halfway through the alley when a slender shape detached itself from a gateway and appeared in front of her. She screamed. Unlike the first encounter, it frightened her; but then, she was so nervous after talking to Fess, *anything* would have frightened her.

"Hey, take it easy," Calvin said. "It's only me."

His habitual scowl was enough to scare anyone, but even in the gray twilight that came so early this time of year, she could see that his eyes were gentle and mild.

"Sorry if I frightened you. Didn't mean to," he said.

She was embarrassed, and explained, "It's all right. I'm just a little nervous after what happened Saturday night. It was so awful."

He nodded. "I know."

She spoke more rapidly, betraying just how nervous she was. "And I was talking to the guys at school today, and I just ran into Fess, and he's mixed up in some wild movement he wants me to join, and—and—I don't know what to believe any more."

To her horror and shame she felt herself giving way to emotion under his kind gaze. He put his hand lightly on her shoulder, and the gentle touch served to release her tears.

"Listen, Calvin," she said, fighting them back, but sniffling, "you've got to be careful. The gang is after you. They think you told the cops on them."

"I know that too," he said calmly. "Why else you think I'm duckin' home through the alley? I ain't no hero. I'm a coward."

163

The humor of this struck her in the middle of a sob; she found herself laughing, coughing and crying all at once, while Calvin patted her energetically on the back. Cowardly Calvin, she thought, who had been so brave that first day the police had come. Her eyes and her nose were both running, but she continued to laugh.

The self-proclaimed coward thoughtfully produced a clean handkerchief.

"I been wanting to come and see you," he said, "but I didn't know whether your mom would let you have company."

"Sure she would," she said, but she felt uncomfortably tense, and all too aware of the light pressure of his arm on her shoulder.

Feeling her stiffen, he withdrew his arm and stepped back a few inches. "That wasn't the reason I didn't come," he confessed. "I just thought you wouldn't be interested in me, on account of all your other boy friends."

She laughed a little at that. "What boy friends?"

"Oh—you know. David, Frank, the whole gang. And that smart boy Fess."

"They aren't my boy friends. They just let me hang around," she explained. Then, remembering what they had told her today, she gave him a troubled sidewise look. "Did you do it, Calvin? Did you tip the cops off?"

He returned her look steadily, his face beginning to tighten in a frown. "Do you think I did?"

She remembered that, for some strange reason, what she thought was terribly important to him. "Oh, no, Calvin, I don't think you did it. I just wondered because I didn't see you around for such a long time."

His lower lip protruded in anger. Calvin's scowl was not really ugly, though; it was almost attractive, like a pouting child's. "I just got tired of seein' all those other guys hangin' around you, if you really want to know why I stayed away. I figured I didn't have a chance. So I thought it would be better if I didn't come around the clubhouse any more."

She was both happy and embarrassed, and didn't know how to reply. Luckily he went on to something else.

"No, it wasn't me told the cops, Lou. It was that older boy, the one that always looks so dirty and scruffy—Roger. They brought him down to the station house the same day they had me there, and put him right in the same cell with me. He just got out of jail last May, for robbery, and they wanted him again for going to D. C. for two weeks and breaking his parole. If he hadn't given them some information, they'd of sent him back to jail. But he's still out, so he must have told them. *You believe me?*"

The last question was asked with great intensity, and a stare like a searchlight.

"Yes!" she exclaimed quickly. Then, shyly, she added, "Calvin?"

He moved closer. "What?"

"I would have invited you over my house before, only it's not much to brag about. Ten people in five rooms. I mean it's never very neat or anything, and I'm sort of ashamed to have company there."

He gave a delighted peal of laughter. *"Five rooms!* Baby, if you only knew how *I* live! Your house would probably look like a palace to me."

She couldn't believe him. "How could it?"

"Don't you remember that time I asked your brother to let me do my drawing at his place, 'cause I didn't have any room to work at home? You think I was kidding? Dig:

"I live with my father. Just him and me. He has this restaurant on the Avenue, a real greasy spoon, and he works long hours in there, fifteen-sixteen hours a day, so he can't live noplace else. We have the restaurant in front, and this one room behind it, about six by ten, with two beds in it and piles of dirty clothes. That's home."

She shook her head in wonderment, thinking of her pointless shame about the little house on Carlisle Street.

"There's two people in that room if you just count my father and me. Three if you count the cat. A *thousand* and three if you count the roaches."

She laughed. For someone who seemed so serious, Calvin was really very amusing when you got to know him.

"And you got *five whole rooms*." He whistled. "Whew! What a lucky girl. Good-lookin' and rich besides."

Giggling, she allowed him to take her hand and swing it as they walked the rest of the way down the alley.

"When am I gonna see this fabulous palace?"

She giggled again. "Oh, any time you want, I guess. . . . What happened to your mother, Calvin?"

She immediately wished she hadn't asked that. He dropped her hand and shoved both of his into his pockets, and his face tightened into its former fierce expression. "She's gone," he said.

"I'm sorry," she replied, thinking he meant that she had died.

"She ran off and left us when I was little. We don't

talk about her much, Pop and I, but he ain't got no use for women. He says you can't trust none of 'em. He's probably right." He gave her an angry look. "This your house?"

"Yes."

He scowled at it with a touch of envy, then asked abruptly, "You got a mother and everything?"

"Yes," she said, and added quickly, "Would you like to meet her?"

He was moving off into the shadows. "Some other time."

"Calvin, wait!"

He turned, a small, lonely figure in the gathering darkness.

"I forgot. I have to ask a favor. Jethro needs blood. Would you go by the hospital and give a pint for him?"

"Oh, wow," he said ruefully, and came closer. "So busy thinking about myself, I forgot all about poor old Jethro. Now there's a guy who's *really* got it rough. Sure I'll go. Right away."

"And Calvin?"

"Yeah?"

She said softly, "You're lucky to have a father. Mine's been gone for years."

"Yeah, well, that's the breaks," he said tonelessly, and touched his cap. "See you, Lou."

"See you."

He disappeared into the black hole of the alley, leaving her with many more things she wanted to say. Like:

Don't blame your mother for leaving, Calvin. Maybe she had a good reason, like my father did. And:

167

Please be careful. Remember the gang is after you. Watch out for them. And, most important of all:

Please don't change your mind about coming to see me. Please come back soon!

But she hadn't had a chance to say any of them, and she was left with a terrible fear that he would stay away now, and an aching sense of loss that was worse than her earlier feeling of not having anything to lose. It was hard not to lose your cool when people had so many ways of warming you. With a look. A touch. A smile.

Or even a scowl.

TWELVE

THE NEXT DAY LOURETTA STAYED HOME FROM SCHOOL TO GIVE
Momma some much-needed rest—and because she didn't
feel like going anyway. With her new attitude, she would
have preferred *never* going to school again. She was much
happier staying home, getting the younger children off to
school and cleaning up the breakfast dishes and mopping
the kitchen floor. After that she straightened the living
room, swept the front steps and took the family wash to
the laundromat—a job Momma had to do every other day.
On her way home she bought a half-pound of bologna and
a big twenty-cent loaf of cottony white bread, and when
she got there it was already time to set them out with mustard and cups of tea for the children's lunch.

They tore through the house like a whirlwind, gob-
bled down their sandwiches in fifteen minutes, and left
the kitchen even messier than it had been that morning,
with crumbs and trash everywhere and streaks of mud dis-
figuring the floor. Louretta sighed and cleaned it all up
again. Then she put an old, tough cut-up stewing chicken
and two onions into Momma's largest pot to simmer all afternoon.

Momma was supposed to be sleeping, but she called out commands every half hour.

"See if the boys got clean underwear!"

There hadn't been any in the wash. Louretta checked Gordon's and Andrew's room and found balled-up sets of dirty underwear everywhere—under the bed, in the closet, between the books in the orange crate they used as a bookcase. And no clean sets in the dresser. The boys left their clothes scattered everywhere; it was impossible to train them to use a laundry hamper. Wondering how William could stand sharing a room with them, Louretta decided against a second trip to the laundromat. She filled the bathtub with hot water, soap and bleach and left the mess to soak for an hour.

"Check the twins' blouses, too!" Momma called.

Clarice and Bernice had identical plaid skirts in two different color combinations which they wore to school on alternate days, and four blouses apiece to wear with them. Louretta found six of these, soiled, stuffed in the corner of what was supposed to be *her* closet. Today the twins were wearing the only clean blouses they owned, without a thought for tomorrow. Her roommates were no better than William's.

Grimly she tossed the blouses into the tub along with the boys' underwear, forgetting about the bleach, and enjoyed a satisfying moment of revenge on seeing all the brightly colored rick-rack trim, carefully chosen to match the skirts, fade to a dreary gray.

"*That'll* learn 'em," she said to herself. Boys were hopeless, but it was time Clarice and Bernice learned to wash their own clothes. And if they thought she was going to *iron* their things, they were sadly mistaken. They could iron them themselves, or wear them rough-dried.

"Louretta, I think I hear that chicken boiling over!"

"Yes, Momma." Louretta ran downstairs to check the pot on the stove. Momma had been right. She turned the flame down under the chicken, set the table for dinner, and warmed a bottle for Cora Lee, who was giving out her hungry cry upstairs. Where was Arneatha? Out shopping, probably. She was the only one in the house who always seemed to have money, Louretta thought resentfully.

The baby fed, she wrung out the clothes and hung them on the lines that were strung across the crowded little bathroom.

Another half hour had passed. Regular as clockwork, Momma called out, "Put some more coal on the furnace!"

Louretta made it to the basement just in time. The fire had almost gone out, but with some energetic poking and rattling followed by two shovelfuls of coal, she managed to revive it. She noted worriedly that the coal bin was almost empty, and hoped this wouldn't be another winter like the last one, when they never had enough cash to buy coal by the ton and had to let the fire burn low, sending one of the boys running to the store for a five- or ten-pound bag of coal at the last minute.

She squatted down beside the warm, friendly furnace to forget about problems and escape into a brief daydream about the future. Someday she would have a good job and an apartment of her own, with no worries about heat—and no messy sisters to share her neat, clean rooms. And no noisy kids, like the ones now rampaging across the floor overhead, to disturb her quiet thoughts.

School was out already—and after peeling ten potatoes, de-stringing two hundred string beans, and making and sweeping under eight beds, she was almost willing to go there herself. Having created new disorder in the living room, the kids ran back outside to play till suppertime. The front room was empty again when William arrived.

"How de do, Sister Lou?" he greeted her with a tired attempt at his customary humor. But his face looked strained and worn.

"How's the mill, Brother Bill?" she replied almost as wearily.

He dropped the pretense of cheerfulness. "Don't ask," he said, and flung himself into the nearest chair. He lit a cigarette, then looked at it and said, "Guess I better give these up. I can't afford them much longer." He stubbed it out in one of Momma's precious painted china dishes, then carefully put the butt back in his pack.

Sensing trouble, Louretta drew a hassock close to his chair and sat down on it. "You look ill, Brother Bill," she rhymed. "What's wrong?"

"They told me today, 'Your services will be terminated as of the 30th.'" He laughed hollowly. "'Your services will be terminated.' That's white folks' language for 'You're fired, boy.' A fancy way of saying, 'We don't need you no more.'"

"Oh, no," she moaned. "Why?"

"I been goofin' up too much, Lou. Getting into work late, missing too many days, falling asleep on the job when I *am* there."

The November wind howled around the house. This could mean no coal at all in the bin this winter—no tons, no half-tons, no five-pound bags. And no chicken of any age. The elderly contents of the pot on the stove were suddenly very precious to Louretta. She ran to the kitchen to make sure the chicken wasn't burning—and to avoid looking at her brother's face.

But she had to come back, and when she did, he gave a nervous start. "Don't scare me like that, Lou. I thought you were running to tell Momma I got fired."

"She's upstairs."

He looked relieved. "Oh. Well, let's not tell her right away, huh? I'm appealing this thing to the Civil Service Board, and I should win—my good record, my seniority, all that. If not . . . well, something else may turn up in the meantime. No sense in getting her upset unless we have to."

Louretta nodded. He hadn't really needed to tell her that. She decided to change the subject. "How's Shirley these days?"

"I thought you knew. I don't see her any more. She wants a man with some prospects," he said bitterly, "and I don't have any."

Louretta sighed. In this conversation, there seemed to be no getting away from William's financial situation.

He relit his cigarette butt nervously and stared into the smoke. "If only I could've kept on with the business. I'd made a good start, Lou. I was beginning to get more printing jobs than I could handle in my spare time, that's why I messed up at work." He shook his head. "I guess it just doesn't pay to try to do two things at once."

Louretta thought of the gang, and said, "It doesn't pay to try to help people, either."

He winced at the hard sound of her voice. "Hey—that doesn't sound like you, Lou."

"Well, I mean it. If you had cooperated with the cops, your printing shop would still be open. Right?"

"I guess so."

"Well, you might as well have. Because those kids thought you were telling on them anyway. They were actually planning to beat you up, until I set them straight."

He leaned forward and put a hand on her knee. "I think I better set *you* straight, Lou," he said. "You don't do things like that for other people. You do them for *yourself*, and that way you've got no kick coming if other people aren't grateful. I couldn't live with myself if I'd given evidence to those cops after what they did to Jethro. If I'd told them about the guns, they'd have been in the clear. They'd think they could come back down here and shoot somebody else any time they felt like it. And the next time, it might be *me*."

Louretta was silent.

"So I did it for *myself*, not for your friends. See?"

Louretta hugged her knees and huddled over them. Then she lifted her head and gave her brother a hard look. "You really think you can get any of those cops punished?"

He lit another cigarette to help him consider that. "No," he said at last. "But I can make them a little more careful how they treat people in the future."

Her short, cynical laugh at this disturbed him. "Lou, I don't understand what's happened to you. You're different."

"I'm growing up, that's all. Faster than you did," she said. She stood up, cutting off all further explanation. "Somebody at the door."

She opened it and stared in surprise at the vision of the steps. She was used to seeing Miss Hodges look nice in school, but seeing her here was something else. You could tell she didn't belong in the neighborhood; her smooth brown skin was the only thing she had in common with the residents of Carlisle Street. Her chic red hat and coat belonged to another world. She came in, bringing a cloud of delicate scent into a room that usually smelled of pork and cabbage.

William was staring in amazement and open admiration as Miss Hodges shed her coat to reveal the trim, matching red wool dress beneath.

"William, you remember my English teacher, Miss Hodges."

"I guess I didn't take a good look that other time," he said, grinning shamelessly. "You know, I was just thinkin' about how I need to brush up on my English. Do you think I could get back in school?"

Miss Hodges considered this question very seriously. "Well, I think you're too old to come in the daytime, but there's the Adult Evening School, you know."

"It's a *joke!*" Louretta exploded, a bit embarrassed by her forward brother.

"Oh, I see." Miss Hodges paused to take this in, then gave a perfectly natural, perfectly delightful laugh.

"Excuse me, ma'am," William apologized awkwardly. "I was just paying you a compliment, in my corny way.

They didn't have teachers that looked like you when I was in school. Uh . . . I guess I'll leave you and Sis alone now."

"No, please stay. This concerns you too. May I sit down?"

William instantly pulled out a chair for Miss Hodges, then sat down on the couch expectantly.

"I'm sorry to surprise you with this visit, but Louretta wasn't in school today, and I didn't want to wait till tomorrow to tell her. I have good news." She turned to Louretta. "Louretta, you know a group of teachers went to City Hall Monday."

Louretta nodded warily; she didn't have much faith in teachers or their power to change things.

"Well, we saw the Mayor and told him about your youth group. He was very interested. He said a group like yours should be encouraged to continue."

"Is he going to give us any money?"

Miss Hodges frowned. "Well, no. At least, not right away. He wants to, but these things take time—meetings, hearings, appropriations . . ." She looked helplessly at William.

"I didn't think he would," Louretta said.

"But in the meantime, you have the money you took in at the dance," Miss Hodges reminded her gently, "and you *still* haven't heard my good news. The Mayor spoke to the Police Commissioner while we were there and got permission for your brother to open again."

She looked past Louretta's somber face to William, who was beaming. "All charges against you have been dropped. They were ridiculous charges, anyway. A non-profit youth group doesn't need a license to hold dances. The Mayor said, instead of being closed up and fined, you ought to be commended."

"When can I open?"

"Right now," she said, and handed him his keys.

William leaped up in excitement. "Miss Hodges," he said shamelessly, "do you mind if I kiss you?"

The teacher kept her poise. "Well, if you're going to do that, you'd better call me Laura."

"A lovely name," he said. He only kissed his hand to her, though. Then he turned, swooped, and planted a noisy smack on Louretta's cheek. She sat unmoved.

"What ails *you*, Sister Lou? Why the sour puss?"

"Can the Mayor make Jethro well?" she said stonily.

All the politicians in City Hall couldn't make Jethro well, any more than all the king's horses and all the king's men could do it for Humpty Dumpty, and the adults knew it. They were silent.

"No, of course he can't," Miss Hodges finally said. "That's the other reason why I came today, Louretta. I wanted to talk to you. Mr. Lucitanno told me some disturbing things about your new . . . er . . . attitude."

"That's right, talk to her," William growled. "She just finished telling me she's growing up. Well, if you ask me, she's growing up *wrong*."

"What do you think is the difference between a child and a grown-up, Louretta?" Miss Hodges asked her.

"Kids believe a lot of nonsense," Louretta answered promptly. "Fairy tales about life—like the stork, and Santa Claus, and all the silly things they teach you in school. Adults know the truth."

"And the truth is that everything in the world is bad. Is that it?"

Louretta nodded bleakly. "Pretty much."

"Well, then, I think you're confused," the teacher said. "Believing in Santa Claus and fairy tales *is* childish. But believing the worst about everything is childish, too. If you become completely negative about life, you don't know the truth, either. You still have some growing up to do."

"The truth is, life isn't all good *or* all bad. It's a mixture, like my day was today. That's the grown-up way of looking at things, Lou," William contributed. "Isn't that right, Miss Hodges?"

"Laura," the teacher corrected with a smile. But she did not take her eyes from Louretta. "Louretta, you're one of the most promising youngsters in my classes. You have every reason to keep striving. But this week you've been showing alarming symptoms of giving up." She lifted her eyes to William's. "You've seen the kids who've given up. I see them every day, and it's no use trying to teach them. They have no hope, no belief in anything. They've quit trying."

He nodded somberly.

Miss Hodges focused her attention on Louretta again. She grabbed her hand urgently. "Louretta, that mustn't happen to you! You have too much to live for. I came to beg you—please don't give up! I wanted to have a long talk with you, but now that I'm here, I think I can sum it all up in those four words. I know things look bad right now, but *please don't give up*. That's all I want to say."

Louretta started to speak, but Miss Hodges released

her hand and held up a warning finger. "No—don't answer. I couldn't bear it if you said 'No' right now. Just think about it, please. I'll see you tomorrow."

After that final remark—a confident statement that showed she assumed Louretta would return to school—she stood up to leave. William helped her into her crimson coat while Louretta watched, wondering whether she would ever own a coat like that. Right now it seemed way beyond her reach.

"Oh, Louretta, I forgot to tell you," Miss Hodges said at the door. "Mr. Lucitanno is very anxious to buy the instruments. Do you think you could bring the money to school tomorrow?"

"I guess so," she said listlessly.

"The class turned in some good papers last month, too. I'm hoping to put the best ones in your newspaper. It should be a wonderful issue, along with your friends' things." She looked at William. "I'd like to meet with everybody who's interested in the paper at the building tomorrow. Right after school, if you can be there to let us in."

"I don't get off work till five, but"—he fished in his pockets—"here, take the keys—and God bless you."

Whistling, he turned from the door after watching Miss Hodges get into her stylish little car. "Some people around here are pretty gloomy," he remarked, "but me, I feel like celebrating. How about a steak dinner?"

"I already made chicken," she told him curtly, and ran to the kitchen to check on it.

All through the meal, she wondered how she was going to slip away after dinner without Momma's noticing, but it turned out to be easy. Momma's sense of responsibility hadn't let her sleep a wink all day, and she was still tired. After dinner, she excused herself and went to bed early. William went out, probably to celebrate with a couple of drinks at one of the Avenue bars, and after the kids crowded into the front room to watch television, Louretta found herself alone in the kitchen. She washed the dishes, then slipped quietly out the back door.

The address Fess had given her was on the other side of town—the North side, a tough district where crimes and killings were common. Before this week she would have been afraid to go there alone at night, but now she hardly cared what happened to her. So, of course, nothing did. She reached the address without incident and knocked on the door.

The shade on the inside of the door's glass panel was pulled aside immediately, and a bushy-haired, bearded face peered out with suspicious eyes. Then the door was opened a crack.

Louretta remembered. "Lumumba," she whispered.

She heard the sound of several locks being unlocked. Then the chain slid out of its socket, and the door was opened just wide enough for her to enter.

"Welcome, Sister," the hairy figure said, carefully replacing the chain and turning latches. He wore a full beard, a toga made of rough cotton, and a string of wooden beads around his neck.

"Go that way. There are a few formalities before you can pass into the meeting." He motioned toward a booth curtained off by hanging sheets.

From the moment his face had appeared inside the door

180

Louretta had felt a creepy feeling of foreboding. When she stepped inside the curtained booth, it was confirmed.

Two girls in flowing cotton dresses and bright head kerchiefs looked up.

"No cigarettes, matches, cosmetics, chewing gum, liquor, or dangerous instruments allowed in the meeting," one recited. "No newspapers or Western literature, either."

"We have to search you for concealed weapons," the other said, and advanced toward Louretta.

Clenching her teeth, Louretta submitted to the indignity of being patted all over by these strange—and strange-looking—girls, but she didn't like it any more than the boys had liked the police search, and she refused to let them go through her purse. Was her nail file a "dangerous object"? Was her *Pocket Book of Poems* "Western literature"? What right did they have to inspect and judge her belongings?

"Just keep it here," she said, taking out her wallet and handing them her large, battered pocketbook. "I'll get it back from you when I leave."

It was a reckless move, but preferable to letting them go through her personal things. That they might do it anyway after she had left the booth occurred to her too late. But, as it turned out, they hardly had time.

The small room was crowded with more colorful people seated on rows of folding chairs. Printed cotton garments seemed to be the rule for both men and women, along with beads and bushy hairdos. The men had the *longest* hair, though. Feeling conspicuous in the plain gray jumper that was ordinarily so inconspicuous, Louretta sat down in the back row.

Another bearded and togaed fellow promptly sprang from the back wall to inform Louretta that females were required to sit on the opposite side.

Louretta complied, but felt her anger rising. She had never encountered so many regulations in her life, not even at school, and she had only been here two minutes! Oh, well. At least she didn't have to sit with Fess, who was grinning at her in an insulting way from the opposite row, as if saying, "At last you've recognized my superior wisdom." Embarrassed, she wished he would look away.

Her wish was finally granted. Fess turned his attention to the small platform at the front of the room, and Louretta did likewise.

The speaker was the most striking figure of all, a tall, blue-black young man with flowing floor-length robes, a pointed goatee, and at least four inches of hair, making him seem eight feet tall. In one hand he held up a piece of mahogany carving—an African mask with snakes instead of hair.

"And I say to you that it is not enough to stop trusting white people! You must stop trusting *anyone* whose skin is lighter than this!"

Louretta was the palest person in the room. The ones in front of her were too polite to turn and stare, and perhaps she only imagined the rustling sound that meant eyes on either side of her were shifting in her direction, but she felt exceedingly uncomfortable.

"White blood corrupts everything it touches," the speaker was saying, "and they have too much of it to be trusted!"

What was it Mr. Lucitanno had said? *Blood is just blood. It's all red.*

She clung to those words as the speaker went on, "As I look around the room, brothers and sisters, it really makes me proud to see so many beautiful black faces, and to see so many dressed in the traditional clothing that sets off their beauty."

Louretta had to agree with him there. Once you got used to the strange costumes, you had to admit that they were very striking, and that most of the people looked handsomer in African dress than they would in drab American-style clothes.

"But I also see a few faces of a lighter hue—and I must admit that I am very suspicious of them. They remind me too much of white faces . . . and I'm *always* suspicious of white faces!"

That did it. While the audience laughed wickedly in appreciation, Louretta wasted no time in getting out of there. She fled into the sheet-curtained booth, snatched her purse from the astonished girls, and ran.

"Leaving so soon, Sister?"

"Won't you give us your name and address?"

"Yes! No!" she shouted over her shoulder, and headed for the front door, anticipating trouble. But the silent, bearded doorman gravely unlocked his six locks for her, and she fled gratefully into the fresh air.

She wasn't sure what those people were up to in there, but it sounded like they wanted revenge. And it seemed that if they couldn't get to the *real* ones they were after, they would pick on the nearest facsimile. *Her.*

She walked up the street, gratefully breathing the cold

183

air. It had been stifling in that meeting. But now she was free!

Her relief was short-lived, though. The clatter of heavily-shod feet, chasing her, rang out clearly in the frosty air. And then a voice:

"Hey, Lucretia! Wait up!"

The fact that Fess could never get her name right was only one of the many things she resented about him.

He caught up to her, panting. "Why'd you leave so soon?"

"I didn't like it."

He stood in front of her, blocking her way with outstretched arms. "But you didn't give it a chance!"

"I heard enough, thank you." She tried to step around him, but his extended arms prevented her. When she gave up, he dropped them.

"Look—I admit that was pretty rough, hearing him put down light-skinned people the minute you walked in. But you have to have an open mind about these things. How are you going to learn anything if you don't listen?"

Taking her silence as a sign that she had relented, he put his arm around her and tried to turn her around.

"Come on, we'll go back and hear the other speakers. They've got some good ones tonight."

His arm was a heavy weight around her shoulders. But when she tried to pull away, it tightened. "Darn it, Fess, let go!"

Even in the dark she could see the instant fury in his face. "Oh, it's like that, huh? It only proves the brother was right tonight. You light-skinned girls all have superiority complexes."

184

"I think it's the other way around," she gasped. "*You* have the complex." But after that she was silent, grimly occupied with the struggle to free herself as he increased the pressure of his arm and forced her back against a shadowy wall.

"You think you're too good for a guy like me. I've run into your type before."

In that moment she saw through Fess, all the way to the bottom of his miserable soul. Some light-skinned girl had rejected him sometime, somewhere—maybe back in Boston, maybe here, and maybe because he was dark, but maybe because he was *unpleasant*—and he had never gotten over it. She pitied him. But at the moment, she was in too desperate a fix herself to waste time pitying others.

"Time you learned," he muttered. "The women in this movement respect us. And they *belong* to us."

He had one arm across her chest, pressing her against the wall, and was breathing hard in her face. She snapped her head from side to side to evade the unwanted kiss he was pressing on her. Then terror struck as she realized that a mere kiss would not satisfy his rage. With his free hand he was attempting to unbutton her coat, and his raised knee was pressing against her legs in an effort to separate them.

But Louretta was a fighter. She bent her head suddenly. Her teeth found the arm that was pinioning her against the wall and bit deeply.

He gave a howl of pain and loosened his grip for an instant. In the next instant she was free, and running for her life.

But he did not chase her. A block away, she slowed down. Behind her, in the dark, she could still hear his sobs.

THIRTEEN

WILLIAM HAD BEEN WAITING UP WHEN SHE GOT IN. GRAVE lines of concern were etched on his broad face.

"Where've you been?" he demanded. "You look like you were in a dogfight."

"William, please," she said. "I'm tired. Let me go to bed."

But he had persisted. "You know you're not allowed out alone at night, Lou. If running wild is your idea of growing up, I guess I'll have to lock you up till you're *really* grown."

Once she would have reacted defiantly, but she had learned a lesson tonight. "William, I promise I'll never sneak out again. Just promise you won't tell Momma. Please."

He looked dubious. "I wish I knew which of those hoods you were out with. I'd teach him to respect my sister."

She was silent. She could never hate Fess again. She could only feel sorry for him.

William was looking at her closely, taking in her disheveled hair, her tearstained face, her torn stockings. He touched her coat in the spot where a button was newly missing, and said awkwardly, "Sis . . . did anybody *do* anything to you?"

"No," she answered instantly. She knew she could never talk about what had happened tonight. Not to anyone. "Nothing happened. Please believe me, William. And please *trust* me. I promise I'll stay home after this."

"Okay," he said finally. "But if you change your mind, let me know. Just tell me who the guy was, and I'll whip him." With clumsy fingers he replaced the end of braid that had come loose from the crown of her head. "My little sister is kind of precious to me, you know."

"So is my big brother to *me*," she said, and gave him a quick hug, then ran upstairs fast, because the tears were threatening to come.

William was gone when she left for school the next morning, and when he returned that evening, he seemed to have decided to honor their pact. Not a word was mentioned about Louretta's escapade the night before, and fortunately Momma had slept through it all.

Maybe William really felt festive, or maybe he only wanted to distract her—but whatever the reason, he declared that night, "I feel like celebrating. Here's ten dollars, Momma. Go out and get steaks for all of us."

William's thrifty mother looked at him suspiciously. "Eight steaks? You gone out of your mind?"

"I want steaks tonight," he insisted. "Let's live like white folks, just this once. My shop is open again, and I feel like celebrating. Do you need more money?"

"No," Momma said, putting on her bowl-shaped blue hat with the pink flowers, the one she wore only to church and on her rare trips to the butcher's.

"You're sure?" he asked. "I don't want no tough old round steaks, now. I want sirloin."

"I got enough," Momma declared, her lips tight with disapproval. "Spending this much on one meal is ruination as it is. It would be enough to feed us for three days, if I spent it *right*."

"Andrew, go with her," William teased. "Make sure she doesn't get round steak or hamburger."

"I know what to buy without any help, thank you," Momma replied. "Stay where you are, boy." She went out muttering about William's extravagance, and probably continued muttering all the way to the store and back, but she bought what he wanted. That night there were fragrant, sizzling steaks on the table for all of them, plus kale flavored with bacon ends, hominy grits, and steak gravy.

For once the children were subdued and orderly at the table, staring at the steaks with enormous eyes, waiting for Momma to say the blessing so they could dive into them.

But before they could, there was another diversion. Arneatha, arriving just in time for dinner, was an even more dazzling sight than the steaks.

She tried to sneak into her place inconspicuously, but in the new outfit she wore, that was impossible. Bright red, obviously brand-new, it featured a three-quarter-length jacket with a collar of rich dark fur which Louretta thought must be mink, although, never having seen mink in her life, she couldn't be sure. Arneatha's skirt was of the same wool fabric, and as she unbuttoned the coat, smiling self-consciously, she revealed a matching blouse. The three-piece suit was almost the same shade as Miss Hodges' outfit, but not quite. This red had a little more orange in it—not much, but enough to make the difference between a rich color and a gaudy one. It was a subtle distinction, but Miss Hodges had looked elegant in her red outfit, while in hers Arneatha looked merely pretty and cheap.

Louretta was envious, though. She thought of her three-year-old cotton coat that was not warm enough for November, let alone the months ahead. She had not mentioned it to Momma because she knew money for clothes was scarce. Yet Arneatha seemed able to acquire new clothes as if by magic.

Tired of being the object of so many stares, Arneatha snapped, "What are you all looking at?"

"If you don't want people to look at you, you shouldn't dress up like a Christmas tree," was Momma's tart comment.

From his high chair, little Randolph spoke for all his brothers and sisters. "You look pretty, 'Neatha."

Arneatha's face softened. "Thanks, baby," she said, and gave him a kiss. "I got a bargain," she explained to the rest of them. "Some guy was going out of business and had a sale. . . . Why don't you all eat?"

But they continued to stare at her. Truly, she was a dazzling sight with the vivid color against her sparkling dark eyes and smooth brown skin.

"Well, I don't know about the rest of you, but *I'm* hungry," she said crossly, and picked up her knife and fork.

As if that had been the signal, everyone else did likewise. Silence followed until every morsel of steak had been consumed. Louretta ate hers so fast she hardly tasted it, yet somehow enjoyed every bite. She had never eaten steak before and hadn't known anything could be so good. By the time she finished eating, she had forgotten all about her sister. Her mind turned to other things.

"Say, William, I just remembered something. I forgot to take the dance money to school today. Miss Hodges said to be sure and bring it tomorrow."

"You might be able to give it to her *tonight* if you hurry, Lou. I think she's still around the corner with some of the kids." Having sucked his steak bone clean, he stood up, wiping his hands on a napkin. "I'll go upstairs and get it for you."

They heard the noise of several drawers being slammed overhead, followed by the banging of other pieces of furniture and a couple of very loud, very unchristian exclamations which caused Momma to tighten her lips. Then William's thumping, uneven steps came rapidly back down the stairs.

He strode into the kitchen and stood over the boys like a tower of wrath. "All right, which of you took that money out of my drawer? 'Fess up, or I'll *really* be hard on you."

Gordon and Andrew sat upright and sturdy in their chairs without cringing from their brother's terrible look.

"I didn't go in your drawer," Andrew said.

"Me neither. No, *sir*," Gordon echoed.

There was something manly and unflinching about their manner that made William hesitate. "I know I put it in a tin can," he said uncertainly. "I thought I put the can in my top drawer, under my socks. But maybe I'd better go look again."

As he left the kitchen, Arneatha slid from her chair, mumbling, " 'Scuse me now, folks. I got a date."

"What's your hurry?" demanded Momma, who hated waste. "You're leaving good food on your plate."

"Not hungry," Arneatha said, and tried to get out of the house fast, wriggling into her new red jacket as she went. But she had made her move a moment too soon. With a gleam in his eye, her giant of a brother stood blocking the kitchen doorway.

"Hold it, Missy," he commanded. "Hold it right there." He looked at her appraisingly. "Say, that's a gorgeous outfit you're wearing."

"Thanks," she said uneasily.

He touched her collar. "Fine fur collar and everything. That's mink, isn't it?"

Arneatha nodded reluctantly.

"I always wonder how come some people in this family can afford such fine new clothes."

"I told you, I got it on sale!"

"On sale, huh? That must have been some sale." He eyed Arneatha up and down thoughtfully, and said, "You know, I know something about clothes. I pushed a garment truck for a while before I got on at the post office. Suits like that cost around a hundred and fifty dollars."

"Lord have mercy!" Momma cried, throwing up her hands at the mention of a larger sum than she had ever possessed in her life.

"Even if the man was having a *half* price sale," William concluded, "or if she got it hot, which I suspect, she'd have to pay at least seventy-five for an outfit like that. How 'bout it? Was it hot, Arneatha?"

"Yes," she admitted with lowered eyes, knowing Momma disapproved of making purchases from the numerous Avenue hustlers who sold stolen goods. But Arneatha's attitude was like that of most of the neighborhood—the hustlers had to have some way of earning a living, and poor people couldn't afford to pay store prices anyway.

"By a strange coincidence," William said, "seventy-five dollars was the amount I had in that can."

There was no use in Arneatha's defending herself; Momma had already reached a verdict. "Take it back, Arneatha," she ordered.

"I can't, Momma," Arneatha cried. "Didn't you hear me say it was hot? The guy I bought it from is probably a hundred miles away by now."

"I won't shelter a thief in my house," Momma said sternly, as if she were quoting from the Bible.

Realizing she had admitted her guilt by her silence, Arneatha tried to retreat to the living room. But William seized her arm and pulled her back.

"Then if she wants to stay, she'll have to find a way to pay it back, won't she, Momma?" he said. "She's been getting away with an awful lot lately. But that's going to end right now. Tomorrow she's going to go out and get a job."

Arneatha was beginning to feel sorry for herself. "I never finished school," she complained. "I can't get any jobs but housework."

"Then do housework," he said unfeelingly. "Momma isn't too good to scrub and clean around here all day. But I notice you seem to feel you're too good to help her. Now, why is that?"

Arneatha's tears were flowing. "You don't know what it's like, having to sit around this ugly old house all the time, wanting to go nice places and have pretty things. It's all right for the rest of you—you don't know the difference. But I *do*—and I can't stand it!"

"Don't be too hard on her, William," Momma said sadly. "It's my fault."

"*Your* fault?" he echoed in astonishment.

"Yes, I blame myself because I let her run wild all those years you were sick. I was so busy taking care of you, I didn't have time for her," Momma explained. "I didn't watch her, or correct her when she was wrong, or iron her little dresses, or anything. I let her grow up wild, and this is my punishment."

Arneatha's eyes were dry again. Louretta thought she saw a faint, calculating gleam appear in them.

"And by the time you got well, her father was gone, and it was too late to do anything with her. I been trying to make it up to her, but I can't."

"You're wrong, Momma. It's not too late," William said quietly. "Strikes me the only mistake you ever made was blaming yourself and feeling sorry for her. She's been working on your sympathy ever since."

Arneatha's eyes blazed at William, and a stream of hot abusive words came from her lips.

"Nice language," he said sourly. "She's been working on your guilty conscience all these years, Momma. Making you believe you owe her something. What about all the things she owes you?"

"I don't owe nobody nothin'," Arneatha said stonily.

William corrected her firmly. "You owe Louretta and her friends the seventy-five dollars they took in at that dance. And you owe it to all of us to start doing your share around here."

His sternness seemed to work on Arneatha. "What do you want me to do?" she asked in a small, penitent voice.

"You can start by changing out of that outfit into something sensible, and cleaning up this kitchen. Momma's not getting any younger, you know. From now on, you help her with the housework and looking after the kids."

She nodded meekly.

"And tomorrow, you go out and look for a job."

Arneatha's face crumpled.

"Look for a job," he repeated, "or leave."

Arneatha hadn't really lost her defiance. "Then I'll leave!" she screamed.

William paid no attention. Acting as if he hadn't heard Arneatha, he turned his back on her and said to Louretta, "I think I still have seventy-five in the bank, Lou. I'll get it out for you tomorrow."

Louretta did not trust her older sister. "What if she doesn't pay you back?"

"She'll pay," he said grimly, "unless she wants to stop eating. Meanwhile, I don't want your friends to be deprived of that money. They've got enough to be mad about already. You know it doesn't take much to set them off, Lou."

Louretta had to admit the truth of this remark. What happened shortly afterward served to emphasize it further. Muttering, "Tired of hanging around this old house anyway," Arneatha got up and left the room. But, inside of a minute, everyone had forgotten about her.

There was a loud banging at the back door, and a hoarse voice cried, "Let me in! Let me in!"

Motioning to them all to stay in their places, William

got up and went over to the door. He paused there, listening. It was a situation that called for caution. People always came to the front door, never to the back one that opened on the alley. It was always locked with three heavy bolts that had grown stiff from disuse.

The pounding continued. "Oh, *please* let me in. Let me in, Lou!" the voice cried desperately.

Hearing his sister's name, William reluctantly slid back the three iron bolts.

A battered, dirty figure in torn clothes tumbled in, staggered two steps, and dropped to its knees at William's astonished feet.

"Gang—jumped me!" he gasped. "About—six of 'em. In the alley."

William bent and helped the victim to his feet. "Why, it's my helper," he said in amazement. "The best one in the whole bunch. Why'd they beat you, boy?"

At the same moment, Louretta also recognized the helpless figure. "Calvin!" she cried in shock. He was so dirty and disfigured she hadn't known him. One badly bruised eye was almost closed, and his head, she noticed now with a sickening feeling, was bloody. Blood was soaking through his woolen cap and running down his collar.

"Jethro died at the hospital," he said. "The gang came after me as soon as they heard. They think I told the cops there was gonna be a fight at the dance."

After the effort of that long speech, his eyes rolled upward and his knees crumpled. William caught him under the armpits just in time to keep him from sagging to the floor again.

Momma, meanwhile, was going into her low, moaning wail. "Poor Jerutha," she said. "Her only boy. Oh, it's a sin and a shame."

"You can cry over him later, Momma," William said with harsh practicality. "Right now you got to look after *this* one."

Momma responded swiftly to this appeal, rising to her feet and snatching up towels. "Lay him on the big bed in the front room, William. Louretta, you heat up some hot water in a basin. Andrew, run to the drug store and get me some bandages."

The older half of the family went into action, while the younger kids, sensing an emergency, stayed out of the way. Momma grumbled continuously: "How a person can raise children in this neighborhood is beyond me. It's enough to break your heart. You just raise 'em up to see 'em struck down." But while she talked, she worked efficiently, removing Calvin's jacket and shirt and trousers, cleaning him up, bandaging him. Soon he had opened his eyes again and was talking.

"A real, full-size bed," he said first in wonderment at finding himself in one. "A real bedroom."

Then he caught sight of Louretta hovering anxiously over him. "Hey," he said with a weak smile, "hope you don't mind if I borrow your mother tonight."

She shook her head to say No, hoping that if she didn't encourage him to talk, he would be quiet and get some rest. He had been badly banged up, with two deep head cuts and a shoulder stab wound as well as a number of bruises. While Mrs. Hawkins worked on his shoulder, he did close his eyes for a moment, seemingly savoring the luxury of having someone take care of him.

But then his eyes flew open again as he remembered something urgent. "Something's up," he said. "They got some kind of plan. You better go around there and check on 'em."

This vague, ominous information delivered, Calvin sank back onto the pillow and went to sleep in earnest. Momma covered him and shushed Louretta and William out of the room.

In the hall, Louretta looked questioningly at her brother, wondering whether Calvin had been temporarily out of his head from the beating he'd received. What he'd said hadn't made sense to her. "Did he mean around at your building?" she whispered. "How would they get in?"

But almost as soon as she'd said it, she remembered.

"Your teacher," William said. "I gave her the keys, remember?"

"Yes, but Miss Hodges wouldn't leave them there alone," she objected. "And they wouldn't do anything wrong if she was there."

"No telling *what* they might do, Lou," he replied grimly. "She's probably gone by now, anyway. But it would have been easy for one of them to hide when she left. Then that one could let all the others in."

Louretta felt a tightening of fear in her chest, knowing it could happen exactly as he'd said. Knowing, too, that in his present state of anger, Fess was liable to be planning anything. *All* of them would be angry and out for vengeance after hearing the news about Jethro. She began to tremble.

"William," she begged, "please don't go around there alone."

"Have to, Lou," he said firmly.

"Then I'm coming with you."

He looked down at her in brief amusement. "You're barely five feet high. You don't weigh a hundred pounds. You really think you'll be much help?"

"You might as well let me," she said stubbornly. "I'll follow you anyway."

When he saw how determined she was, he let her come along.

FOURTEEN

COMPARED TO THE REST OF THE BRIGHT, NOISY AVENUE, THE building seemed reassuringly dark and quiet when they arrived. Four patrol cars were parked on the block, too, making disorders unlikely. Louretta, peering in the front window, saw nothing but blackness at first, and was relieved.

But then a tiny light flickered inside. It glowed only for a moment, then disappeared in the shadow. Had she really seen something, or had she imagined it? Louretta wasn't sure, but she gripped William's arm.

"Careful, William!" she whispered. "I think someone's in there with a candle."

William, trying his extra set of keys in the door, found that they weren't necessary. With a little pressure, the unlocked door swung open, and they slipped inside.

At first Louretta could see nothing in the darkness, but as her eyes grew accustomed to it, she began to make out numerous dark shapes moving stealthily about. Across the room, a flashlight snapped on for a second, and she had the sudden, terrifying impression that there were dozens of the shapes, all tiptoeing about on some mysterious, sinister business. Like a gathering of witches or demons at midnight.

"Flash that light over here a minute, man," a hoarse, familiar voice called from the corner. It was David!

William responded boldly by turning on the overhead bulb to reveal, not demons, but Louretta's familiar classmates. David. Frank. Ulysses. And a number of others who were not so familiar.

Frank was the only one who kept his presence of mind, perhaps because he had not noticed the newcomers. "Hey, cut those lights!" he hollered. "The cops might be watching."

The others, caught by surprise, backed nervously into one corner, eyes blinking at the light. They seemed to be trying to hide something.

Then Louretta sniffed the sharp, pungent odor of gasoline. "Look in the corner, William!"

He strode to the corner, Louretta following. There they found a large metal gasoline can and dozens of the pop bottles that had been emptied and left behind at the dance. The necks of half the bottles were stuffed with rags. One whiff told William all he needed to know.

"You guys planning to burn down this building?" he demanded.

"If necessary, yes," came a cool answer from behind him.

Louretta and William both turned in the direction of the voice to find Fess standing arrogantly in the doorway that led to the back room. Curtains between the two rooms had been improvised with two blankets, but Fess had parted them with his shoulder, revealing that the lights in the back room were burning. Some kind of secret activity was going on back there.

William pushed past Fess roughly, shoving him aside with one hand, and Louretta followed in his wake.

The back room, William's workshop, looked as if a dozen playful monkeys had been turned loose in it. Splotches of spilled ink, pieces of broken type, grease spots, and crumpled papers were everywhere—on the tables, on the press, all over the usually neat and clean floor. Evidently the boys had been trying to operate the press, and their first attempts had not been too successful.

"That's what you get for beating up Calvin," Louretta told Fess scornfully. "He's the only one of you who knows how to run this thing."

"We don't need him," he told her, and produced a smeared sheet of newsprint to prove it. It was messy and stained, but legible. Scanning it quickly, she read the headlines:

COPS COMMIT CHILD MURDER

SOUTHSIDE BOY VICTIM OF RACIST KILLERS

LOCAL PEOPLE REMEMBER JETHRO AS GOOD BOY

DON'T LET THIS HAPPEN TO YOUR KIDS!

In the center of the page, enclosed in a black border, was a series of verses. It was a poem entitled "Lament for Jethro" and signed, simply, "By One of His Friends."

Louretta strongly suspected which one of his friends it was, and as she looked at Fess and recoiled from the seemingly permanent sneer that was stamped on his face, her feelings were terribly mixed. He had such a negative view of things—the kind of outlook Miss Hodges had called another way of being childish—and he certainly wasn't very likable. Yet he had so much intelligence, so much *talent* that might be put to good use . . .

She glanced at the first few lines of the poem and became excited, the way she always did when she read something good. They described Jethro so beautifully tears came to her eyes.

She had a sudden, crazy urge to do something to *help* Fess. It didn't make sense, considering the way he had treated her just the night before. Except for a sixth sense which told her that this boy, unless he obtained some kind of satisfaction at some point in his life, would be capable someday of destroying her and everyone else in the room.

"How you like our special edition?" he asked sarcastically. "It isn't exactly what your little schoolteacher pal had in mind."

At that moment she caught sight of a trim red leather portfolio that she recognized as belonging to Miss Hodges. It had been thrown carelessly on the floor amid the ink and the grease.

"How'd you get that?" she asked fearfully.

"Oh, she left it here," he said carelessly. "She left thinking we were gonna print her nice little English-class essays. But we've got a surprise for her."

Was he telling the truth? Louretta thought of Calvin, unconscious at home in Momma's bed, and wondered if the gang had done anything to Miss Hodges. She knew she had made a dangerous error with Fess by bringing in a teacher who was not even from his school to take control of the newspaper away from him. If there was anything Fess couldn't stand, it was being robbed of his authority. Had it made him angry enough to harm Miss Hodges? She had no way of knowing until later. She took a chance and followed her original impulse.

"It looks good to me, Fess," she said, noting his surprise as she handed the paper back to him. "I think you ought to print it."

But William did not go along with her, and voiced his disagreement most emphatically. "Over my dead body!" he roared. "I want this place cleared out in two minutes flat. Everybody *out!* That means all of you. If you do anything in here tonight, you'll do it over my dead body." His face was working and twitching in rage as he surveyed his littered workroom. Louretta had never seen him so furious before.

"Well, if that's the way you want it, man . . ." Fess said with a sinister little half-smile, and gave a signal. A giant figure stepped from the shadows to pinion William's arms.

Louretta, astonished, recognized LeRoy Smith, also known as "The Bear," gang-boss of the Avengers, the Hawks' arch enemies. His nickname aptly described his appearance—huge hulking shoulders, a great shaggy head, long, dangling, powerful arms. William struggled, but LeRoy was stronger. He had William in a grip from behind that must have been like an iron vise.

To make William's situation worse, a second, smaller boy, one Louretta had never seen before, ran over and held a small, gleaming switchblade just beneath William's chin. At this, her brother stopped struggling. But his eyes continued to blaze like two angry fires.

"The Avengers came in with us on this," Fess explained, noticing Louretta's confusion. "The gangs made a truce. We got a common enemy now."

Louretta realized again how dangerous it was to underestimate this boy. It took a genius to get Avengers and Hawks to cooperate.

"Who's the enemy?" she asked, though, in her sickened heart, she knew the answer. To Fess, it was every white person in the world, as well as any person of *any* color who crossed him or disagreed with him.

But he was too busy giving orders to his confederates to pay her any more attention. Glancing at his watch, he said, "The Man goes off duty at nine. It's seven now. We got two hours to catch him. At eight-fifteen, Hoss and Frank and Roger go in the alley and start raising Cain to draw him into the ambush. You other guys, be ready to jump him."

He paused to grin briefly at William. "Too bad the Bear's tied up for a while. We need some muscle for this job." Looking around the room, he picked out the next largest boy. " 'Lysses, you go in place of him. Take somebody extra if you want. I want the Man *wasted*."

The grim directions were clear. They were actually planning to beat up Officer Lafferty, the man who had the entire neighborhood terrorized. Louretta's feelings were uncomfortably divided. Half of her yearned for revenge for what had happened to Jethro, while the other half was repelled by the thought of still more violence. It was like being two people.

Fess continued his careful instructions. "Remember, first thing you do is get his gun off him. Throw it as far away as you can. Don't try to hang on to it. We can't take no chance of getting anybody else killed. How are the cocktails coming?"

David, his face poking as if disembodied through the curtains, a good foot above everyone else's, said, "About half done."

"Good. Hustle 'em up, Hoss. The rest of us got to get these papers out. With all these interruptions, we may only have time to print a few hundred. But that's enough. We got other ways to make sure everybody gets our message."

"Darn right," said the wiry boy who was holding the knife on William.

Fess continued, "When you're through with The Man, separate and spread out as far as you can. I want every window from here to Fourth Street smashed. And every building burning. Who's distributing the papers?"

A half-dozen hands waved eagerly.

"We won't have many, so spread 'em around as much as you can. Try to get a couple on every block in Southside. After you've finished, you know what to do next."

Forgetting the need for caution, the boys yelled loudly:

"Yeah, man!"

"*We* know!"

"Just watch us!"

They danced about in glee, while their leader beamed a truly fiendish smile of triumph.

But he had made the mistake of forgetting about Louretta. She looked so small and harmless that the leader of a gang of man-sized boys might well feel he could afford to ignore her presence. But he had forgotten that her petite frame enclosed a voice of heroic proportions.

Slipping unnoticed through the curtains, she raced to the front door and raised her full voice in a blood-curdling, earth-shaking scream. Reaching one hand behind her, she found the knob and opened the door so the sound of her next yell would travel all along the street.

But it only took one to bring all of the boys racing into the front room on the double.

"Don't touch me," she warned as they closed in. "I'll yell some more if you do. And the police are right outside. Lots of 'em."

The boys moaned and complained bitterly, but fell back.

Louretta's emotions took over then. Tearful, half sobbing, she said, "How can you help people by burning down their houses? And my brother's place, too, after he's been so nice to you? It's crazy. It doesn't make sense."

It was the wrong kind of appeal. The boys shuffled their feet and muttered resentfully. In another moment they might come after her.

William, who had been able to get away from his captors in the excitement following Louretta's scream, was alarmed. "Get out of here, Lou," he ordered. "The door's open. Run while you've got a chance."

But Louretta had become calm again. She could make her voice very small and quiet when she wanted to, and it was that way now.

"No, William," she told him firmly. "The door is open so that the *next* next time I yell, the cops will be sure to hear me."

At that, Fess made a threatening move toward her.

"I can make a lot of noise before you shut me up," she warned him quickly. "Enough to get fifty cops in here."

"You hear that, men?" Fess cried. "I always knew she was the kind of chick who would sell her people out to their enemies."

Angry murmurs followed that statement. But Louretta was no longer afraid.

"You don't know who your enemies are," she told him, and turned to stare directly at the tall, skinny boy, once so ragged and disheveled, who was now the best-dressed member of the group. "Why don't you ask Roger what he was doing down at the police station that day they had Calvin there?"

Her target made a sudden dash for the door, but didn't get very far. Two of the gang members restrained him before he could take three steps. Trapped, Roger stood in their unfriendly embrace, his eyes shifting nervously around the room.

"He won't tell you, but I will," Louretta continued. "He was saving himself from going back to jail for breaking his parole. *He's* the one who told them there would be a fight at the dance, not Calvin."

The boys looked skeptical. But her mind was inspired, and racing. "If you don't believe me, why don't you ask him where he got the money for those new clothes? That sweater, and that suede jacket. And how he paid for that process on his hair? He hasn't worked in a year."

The boy with the switchblade knife had a new hostage now. "Speak, rat," he said, brandishing his blade beneath Roger's chin.

But the frightened Roger, his mouth open like a drowning fish's, could only produce a series of gasps. "Uh —uh—uh."

"I bet he's *still* working for the cops," Ulysses said.

"Once a pigeon, always a pigeon," said Frank.

"Yeah, and they pay well for information," David added.

"So he's probably told them what you're planning tonight!" Louretta cried triumphantly. "That's why I saw so many of them on the street outside. They're just waiting for you to make your first move. Waiting for you to break the law."

"Then they'll arrest all of you," William concluded for her. "Not without smashing a few heads first, though. If you boys try something tonight, The Man won't get wasted. *You* will." He scanned the angry, confused young faces and said sarcastically, "How many of you want to end up like Jethro? Any volunteers? Speak up."

"Ah, don't listen to these Toms, men." Fess growled. "They're lying. Let's get on with our plan."

But LeRoy The Bear had a more immediate plan. He grabbed Roger by the lapels of his expensive jacket. "Did you tell, mustard plaster?" he asked, slapping the unfortunate victim on both cheeks, knocking his head from side to side. "Did you? Did you? Huh?"

"Speak, rat," intoned the ghoulish little Avenger with the knife. "Speak or die."

The sound that came from Roger's mouth was like the croak of a dying frog. "Yeah," he admitted. "I—told. Everything."

The Bear's paw hit Roger's nose with a loud crack, and with a roar, the other boys piled in. Louretta kept silent for a short while, knowing they had to take it out on somebody, but half a minute of the beating was all she could stand to watch.

"Stop it!" she cried in a voice that threatened to expand into a full-blown scream. "The cops will hear you!"

The warning worked. The noise subsided quickly, and the boys moved aside reluctantly to reveal Roger with one fist to his eyes, wiping away the tears that were mingling with blood from his nose.

"Let him go," Louretta commanded, not knowing how she had managed to get control of this unruly group, but knowing it had happened.

With a push from The Bear, the sniveling, bloodied stool pigeon lurched toward the door. Once outside, he broke into a run. Louretta was careful to keep the door open wide for protection after he was gone. But the cold air that came through it seemed to bring some of the boys to their senses.

"Guess we better call it off," David said sadly.

"You know it, if the fuzz is hip to our program," Frank replied.

"Sure they hip," said Ulysses. "That guy's a stone stool pigeon if I ever saw one. The kind that would sell his grandmammy's false teeth to the cops and give her a green apple."

Louretta had to laugh at this figure of speech, and so did several others.

But Fess was not amused. He stood apart from the

group with his eyes lowered and his mouth set in a hard line. Everyone else had temporarily forgotten about him. But Louretta was not going to make that mistake again.

Looking straight at Fess, she suggested, "You can still put out the paper."

"Over my dead—" William began.

Louretta interrupted him. "It's a good idea, William! Please let them do it. They have to do *something*."

She knew these kids better than William did. They had to have some kind of outlet for their anger, or they would explode in all directions.

But William shook his head stubbornly. "Not on *my* press," he said. "I'll never let them near it again."

The brief flame of hope that had flickered behind the tortoise-shell glasses died quickly. Fess's eyes returned to their customary hardness and became opaque, difficult to read. Behind them, his active mind might already be at work on a new plan for vengeance.

Louretta had won an amazing victory tonight, but she felt defeated. She walked aimlessly around the room, stopped at the piano, ran a finger listlessly down its yellowed, uneven keys.

"There must be something we can do to remember Jethro," she said half aloud, half to herself. "Something besides fighting and beating up people and killing. There's been too much of that already."

But no one had any suggestions. Not knowing what else to do, Louretta sat down at the piano and played Blind Eddie's three basic chords. Each time she played them, they formed a different pattern, and tonight, for some reason, they reminded her of the hymn Blind Eddie had taught them. Still playing the chords, she picked out the melody with one finger:

> God be with you,
> God be with you,
> God be with you until we meet again. . . .

Ulysses was not really a mean boy. Tough, yes—all Southside boys *had* to be tough—but not mean. Louretta had noticed that big, strong boys seldom were. It was usually the little, puny ones who were meanest. Kindhearted Ulysses was probably relieved that he did not have to beat up Officer Lafferty tonight. At any rate, the second time around, his bass voice, big and comforting, boomed out the words of the hymn close to her ear:

> God be with you,
> God be with you,
> God be with you until we meet again.

But they were the only ones singing. The rest of the room was oppressed by a heavy silence.

"Go 'head, girl," Ulysses said encouragingly when they had finished. "You'll save our souls yet."

She laughed.

David spoke up hesitantly. "You know 'Just a Closer Walk With Thee,' Lou?"

She shook her head regretfully. Oh, she knew the hymn—everybody did—but she didn't know how to play it.

"Try," David urged. It seemed very important to him.

So she did, and found that the old, familiar hymn could be played with the chords she knew. As she grew surer of herself, she gave it more volume and a swinging beat. Several voices joined in:

> Just a closer walk with Thee,
> Grant it, Jesus, if you please . . .

Soon even The Bear was singing, in a thin, squeaky, off-key tenor that did not go at all with his huge, fearsome frame. But to Louretta's ears, it was beautiful.

Fess provided the only sour note, after they finished. "I've had enough of this religious bull. If the cops came in now, they'd laugh at us. Singing hymns like a bunch of old women."

He spat on the floor to show his contempt and started for the door.

But Louretta was not going to let him walk out completely frustrated if she could help it. Not again.

Before Fess reached the door, she caught Ulysses' and David's attention. " 'Hungry Cat Blues,' " she whispered. "One, two, three—"

By the second line, Fess had turned back, recognizing his own words. He stood by the door, listening to the rest of the number in a kind of happy trance. At the end, his face was more relaxed then Louretta had ever seen it, and its broad smile contained no mockery. It was incredible, but he was not quite so ugly any more.

"Applause for the author!" she cried. "Fess, take a bow!"

Obviously uncomfortable, he offered two short, brusque duckings of his head in response to the loud applause—and said, almost to himself, "I never thought about how it would sound to music. It sounds *good*. It's got *soul*."

Even William was impressed by their swift change of mood and their artistry, impressed enough to change his mind. He spoke up awkwardly. "Anybody wants to learn how to run that press now, I'm ready to show 'em."

Fess gave him a slow, amazed, you-must-be-kidding stare. "You mean, so we can run off the paper?"

"Why not?" William said.

Fess gave out a whoop and grinned. Most of the boys joined him and William in the stampede to the press room, but the small singing group remained with Louretta at the piano. Frank, David, Ulysses. Only one face was missing, and Ulysses brought up a painful reminder of that fact.

"We really needed you on that number, Lou," he said. "With Jethro gone, we ain't got no high tenor no more. You're the closest thing to a tenor we got left."

FIFTEEN

"YOU'LL JUST HAVE TO TRY AND UNDERSTAND, ROSETTA," MRS. Jackson said to Louretta's mother. "The Methodist church was never my *true* church, anyhow. I tried to get used to it up here because all my friends were in it, and it was supposed to be more refined. But I always missed the kind of shouting services we used to have down South.

"And at my boy's funeral," she concluded, with a defiant glance that took in the entire party of friends and relatives in her living room, "I want plenty of shouting. I don't want nobody to hold nothin' back. I want shouting that'll be heard all the way downtown at Police Headquarters. And cryin', too. And testifyin'. And some old-fashioned, soul-stirrin' preachin'."

"All right, Jerutha. It's *all right*," Momma said, trying to comfort the little woman, who had burst into tears again. It was the tenth time she'd had to reassure Mrs. Jackson that nobody blamed her for deciding to hold the funeral at Reverend Mamie Lobell's new church instead of at the Methodist Tabernacle, where she was a member.

"I was born a Baptist, and I may *stay* a Baptist from now on," Mrs. Jackson added defiantly. "It's more of a

214

comfort to me than those cold religions. To me, going to a Baptist church is like going home."

"All right, Jerutha, all right," Momma soothed automatically. "Do whatever makes you feel best."

"I wouldn't feel right if I just had a Methodist preacher to say a few cold words over my boy. I want him sent home to Glory with Amens and shoutin'. I hope you understand, Rosetta."

"Yes, yes, I understand. Sure I do. Nobody blames you, Jerutha." Momma dabbed at the little woman's cheeks. "Let me put some more powder on you. You've got your face all streaked again."

But Mrs. Jackson scorned such attentions. "I'm gonna put a lot *more* streaks on it before this day is over. I mean to cry so loud the Lord above will hear me. And *keep* cryin' till them policemen are punished." And she gave a demonstration so loud and contagious that several of the women who were present joined her.

Mrs. Jackson was not alone in her feelings. She had a lot of sympathizers—not just the people in the room who knew and loved her, but hundreds of people all over the neighborhood who had read about Jethro in the boys' newspaper. They had printed five thousand copies that night and distributed them the next day. Those who received papers passed them on, and those who didn't get a chance to read one heard all about the incident from those who had.

Louretta had worked most of that night to help the boys get out the paper, without stopping to read it thoroughly until the next day. In the ensuing days she had spent all her spare time working on something else. Every after-

noon and evening she had gone to the building to meet Blind
Eddie, Frank, Ulysses and David. Except for a word to
Reverend Mamie Lobell, they told no one what they were
doing. Louretta was sure the black choir robe she wore today would give the project away. But no one said anything
about it. Perhaps they assumed she was wearing it because
she could not afford to buy a black dress and were too tact-
ful to mention it. In any case, Mrs. Jackson paid no attention
to Louretta's costume, and the others were too respectful
of her bereavement to comment on anything she hadn't noticed.

Now, looking frail and worn but utterly indomitable,
the little woman stood up, flung her black veil forward
over her face, took William's arm, and announced that it
was time to leave for the church. The twenty others who
had been crowded into the small living room followed.

Only close friends and family were present at the
Jackson house before the funeral, but that added up to a
large number: Jethro's two married older sisters, their hus-
bands and children, and the considerable family of Mrs.
Jackson's best friend, Louretta's mother. Calvin, who was
practically an adopted member of the Hawkins family by
virtue of having spent a week recovering at their house,
was present too. He still bore a number of ugly scars and
bruises, and seemed shaky when he got to his feet, but he
was much less pale. His father, a tall, eagle-faced man with
a thick head of gray hair, had visited him daily and was taking him home today after the funeral.

Children were supposed to wear white at Baptist fu-
nerals, and the twins looked so angelic in their identical
white dresses that no one would believe what devils they

really were. Randolph, a cherub in a white suit with short pants, was also amazingly well behaved. It had been decided that Gordon and Andrew were too old to wear white, and they looked handsome and proud in their good dark suits, and almost as manly as their brother William, whom they resembled more and more. Louretta was very proud of her family that day.

Only one Hawkins face, the prettiest, was missing. They had received a post card that morning from Chicago, saying that Arneatha was working as a waitress there until she could save up enough money to take her to Hollywood. Once there, she felt sure, she would find work in the movies. The card had said nothing about Cora Lee, who of course remained in Momma's care.

So now there was a spare bed in the little house. The night Calvin arrived, Momma had moved it into Louretta's room along with the little ones' cribs so Calvin could have a room all to himself to recover in. Six in a room was terribly crowded, even if two of them were very little, but Louretta had found sharing Arneatha's bed with Momma much more comfortable than sleeping with her restless, energetic, and rapidly growing twin sisters. Now that Calvin was going home, Momma would have her own bed back, and perhaps Louretta would be able to keep Arneatha's. She fervently hoped so.

Climbing out of the long, black limousine at the church, she remembered why they were there and felt ashamed of her selfish preoccupations. The church was so crowded that the ushers at the doors were turning people away. To her surprise she noticed a number of newspaper photographers and TV cameramen in the large, disappointed crowd that milled outside. Several of the photographers took pictures of Mrs. Jackson arriving. One even stepped forward and asked her to lift her veil.

"Will it help punish the men who killed my boy?"

"It might, ma'am," the photographer said.

"Then I'll do it," she said, and flung the veil back and posed until he had taken a picture of her tearstained face. Then the procession moved on. The family party was admitted to the church, of course, but many other mourners were turned back. Reverend Mamie's new church, a two-story stucco building with small stained-glass windows and a single spire, was nice in a plain way Louretta admired, but it was not large enough to hold the hundreds who wanted to get in.

Hundreds were already packed inside. Those who had come too late to get seats were standing at the back and along the walls. More photographers and TV men were inside, too. Louretta tripped on one of the TV cables and almost fell as she followed Momma up the aisle, but recovered her balance in time. When the usher lifted the black rope to let them into the family section at the front, she stood aside.

Momma looked around questioningly, but Louretta smiled and whispered, "It's all right, Momma. I'm sitting up there."

Without further pause she turned and marched up the altar stairs, past the bier that was banked with enough flowers to fill ten greenhouses, to the choir loft, and took her seat beside Ulysses, Frank and David. She was glad that the mass of flowers hid the body from her view; she wanted to remember Jethro alive. But she had a complete view of the congregation, and realized she had never seen so many people assembled before. Looking out over the massed faces below her, she saw numerous patches of white in the sea of brown. A few of the white faces were familiar to her from the newspapers, but she did not know their names until Ulysses pulled the sleeve of her robe and began pointing them out.

"That's the Mayor there in the fifth row. And the Police Commissioner beside him. The other guy is Chairman of City Council." Two rows behind these officials she recognized Mr. Lucitanno, Miss Hodges, a number of other teachers, and the principal of Southern High. School must have been let out for the day because many of Jethro's classmates were present too.

But how, she wondered, had all those other people known about Jethro's funeral? Then she remembered the newspaper. It must have circulated even more widely than they had hoped. Looking at the dignitaries again, she was seized by a moment's panic. She had not expected to be in the spotlight in front of so many important people.

But it was not long before Louretta became engrossed in the sermon and forgot all about herself.

Reverend Mamie did not disappoint Mrs. Jackson or anyone else in her swollen congregation. A two-hundred-pound woman dressed in a black velvet robe, with her impressive gray hair piled high on her head, she was an imposing sight in the pulpit. She had a deep, powerful, expressive voice to match her figure. And it was naturally loud: where other people raised their voices for emphasis, Reverend Mamie had to lower hers.

She began softly and sedately enough, speaking of the

dead boy and reminding her audience that they, too, were mortal and doomed to share his fate.

This drew the first subdued moans and "Amens" from those members of the congregation who had recently had reason to think about this subject. But their reactions were mild in comparison to what followed.

But this boy had suffered an untimely death, Reverend Mamie went on. A cruel death. An *outrageous* death. Cut down before he had even reached manhood!

Moved by this outrage, she began to shout and moan and cry, and the congregation was not long in joining her. Louretta stared in amazement as Reverend Mamie jerked about the pulpit, waving her arms and shouting, and scattered members of the congregation leaped from their seats in response to her exhortations. Most of them remained in their places, screamed once or twice, and settled back in their seats. But several, including both men and women, ran to the aisles and began jiggling in a sort of ecstatic dance that reminded her of Jethro's nervous fits. They were not performing any more than he had been; they were sincere, and in some kind of trance. One man fell on the floor and rolled back and forth, and a woman fainted and had to be helped outside by an usher.

Louretta was appalled. She felt that this sort of religion was very undignified and not at all proper at a funeral. She herself would never indulge in such antics in church.

But a minute later, she was astonished to find that she was on her feet and that one of the voices screaming, "Yes, Lord!" was hers.

Reverend Mamie, huffing and puffing, tears and sweat

pouring down her cheeks, cried "Is this God's justice? To strike down innocent children?"

"No!" the congregation roared.

"But God's voice will be heard in this city! And His justice *will prevail!* Can I get a witness? Who will testify?"

Jethro's mother got to her feet.

"Speak, Sister Jackson."

"I want to testify to God's goodness and love. He saved me many years ago, in my youth, and though I have strayed from the fold many times, He has saved me again and again. And I know He will save the soul of my innocent son."

"Amen," Reverend Mamie said, and was answered by a chorus of Amens from the front rows. "Can I get another witness? Who will testify? What about some of his friends?"

That was the signal. On the front row of the choir loft, Louretta and the three boys stood up in their robes, while at the piano, Blind Eddie began a stately, gospel-style introduction that was like the rolling of thunder. He had set Fess's poem, "Lament for Jethro," to gospel chords because, as he explained, "It ain't exactly a hymn, but these chords'll make it sound like it belongs in church. Besides, I like them with these words."

He was truly a remarkable musician—from jazz and blues, he could switch in a moment to religious music. But Blind Eddie didn't consider this remarkable; in fact, he didn't see much difference among the three types of music. When Louretta had commented on his versatility, he had said, "Shucks, all the best musicians started out in the church. Didn't I tell you that it's where all our music came from? Besides, my daddy was a preacher, and there'd be something wrong if I *couldn't* play church piano."

Now, backed by his rolling, thunderous chords, the four put their heads close together for better harmony and lifted their voices in Fess's words:

Let me tell you 'bout a little guy
Who lived a little while and had to die.
Jethro Jackson was his name.
Since he's gone, things ain't the same.

He never got straight A's in school,
And half the time, he played the fool.
Playing the fool was his favorite part,
But he had heart!

He played tricks on lots of folks,
But there wasn't no meanness in his jokes.
He wasn't in church when they called the roll,
But he had soul!

Now, Jethro never did nothin' great,
But he was a cat you'd appreciate.
He could laugh and sing and fight and dance,
And he might've done more if he'd had the chance.

But just because he showed no fear,
A big cop blew him away from here.
Yes, just because his skin was brown,
A big policeman shot him down . . .

They were really reaching the congregation, Louretta noticed during the rhythmic bridge which Blind Eddie played between each of the verses. People all over the church had been moved to shout their comments, and a number who had been sitting were standing in the aisles. Even white people who had never known Jethro Jackson had their handkerchiefs out and were using them.

Blind Eddie's playing quieted down suddenly as he struck the introductory chords for the next-to-last verse, and the four singers followed suit, lowering their voices to such a soft pitch that the dramatic change brought fresh cries from the emotional congregation:

> Lots of people don't know or care,
> But if there's a Heaven, I know he's there.
> And if he ain't—one thing I know,
> It's no place I want to go,
>
> 'Cause if they'd keep Jethro out, I fear
> Heaven must be just like here.
> Yes, if they'd keep Jethro out, I fear
> Heaven must be just like here.

Louretta had worried all week about how church people would react to those last few lines, which seemed to question their strongest beliefs. But Blind Eddie solved the problem by giving them no time to think about it. Applause was not customary in church anyway, so he did not pause for it, but kept playing, moving, with a sudden shift in key and a deafening increase in volume, into the opening bars of "God Be With You Until We Meet Again."

The four young singers followed his cue, and behind them, the massed choir of forty voices rose to its feet and joined in.

"Everybody!" Reverend Mamie called, raising her arms commandingly. "Everybody, now."

And suddenly all the people in the church were on their feet and singing.

When the hymn had been sung once, Blind Eddie continued playing it softly, and to this accompaniment, Reverend Mamie preached the quiet closing words of her sermon:

"We don't none of us know where we'll meet again, except in Glory. No, we may see a friend in the morning . . . and that same friend may be gone by nightfall. But we know we'll see that friend again someday, when we have passed over too . . . and that we'll see our family and our other dear ones at the same time. So I say today to the family and friends of this boy: Grieve not, be joyous, remember that he has just gone home . . . and that you will join him by and by. God be with you *all* until we meet again!"

And then, to the notes of the hymn sung softly by the entire choir, the casket was carried from the church and followed by the mourners. Louretta, watching, felt exhausted, drained, wrung out, yet somehow peaceful. She knew now why Mrs. Jackson had not wanted a polite, formal atmosphere at Jethro's funeral. There was something about shouting and tears and other extreme displays of deep emotion that satisfied your—your—

There was no other word for it but *soul*.

SIXTEEN

THE WORK OF A CLEVER ARTIST DECORATED ALMOST EVERY fence and telephone pole on Louretta's way from school to the building a week later. Some very talented person had done accurate caricatures of Fess—the pugnacious jaw, the round nose, the bulging eyes behind the huge glasses—and labeled them with libelous captions. "The Dictator," "Adolf Hitler," "The Gangster," and "Al Capone" were only a few. On the pole in front of the building, a beautifully lettered sign said simply, "Down With Dictators." No picture.

She went inside, laughing to herself, to find Fess just getting to his feet, rubbing a sore jaw, and Calvin standing over him.

"Hi, Lou," Calvin said, and jerked a thumb at his victim. "This guy thinks he's an art critic. He objected to the way I did his portraits. Now, you know I'm very sensitive. I can't stand to have my work criticized."

On his feet again, Fess said, "Why, you little—" and swung a mean right at Calvin.

But Calvin intercepted it with his left hand, then banged his right into Fess's eye. Fess sat down again, hard.

Calvin's cheeks were glowing from the exercise, but he was not even breathing hard. Evidently he had made a full recovery.

"Guess I'll run along now, Lou," he said with one of his rare, winning smiles. "I'm sorry to be rowdy in the clubhouse, but I just had to get even with that guy. I'll gladly pay the fine."

Louretta sighed as he left. She was glad Calvin had regained his strength so quickly, but it was going to be hard to get used to seeing him less often. Having him around the house had been a constant joy. Every night, after she brought up his supper tray, they had had long, intense conversations about books and school, friends and parents, past childhood days, plans for the future, and everything else that was important to them. She had grown very fond of this boy who only remembered his mother as "somebody soft," who had discovered his talent for art by lettering signs for his father's restaurant ("It's a real classy joint. You know the kind—'Neck Bone Platter, 35¢.'"), who could laugh and make jokes about all the miserable facts of his life, yet be intensely serious about his work and enthusiastic about his far-fetched dream of going to art school.

Oh, well, she thought with a little laugh, if he keeps on like this, fighting every member of the gang who beat him, he'll soon be under Momma's care again.

The fine was a new rule William had proposed. The group had agreed that members would pay fifty cents into the club treasury for each incident of "fighting, swearing, or general rowdy behavior." David was supposed to be the treasurer, but for some reason, he kept asking Louretta to hold the money. Perhaps he didn't trust himself with it—David was usually broke. At any rate, she'd already collected four dollars this week, and it was only Tuesday, which showed what a rough bunch her friends still were.

But they were improving. Fess, getting wearily to his feet for the second time, bore his humiliation and his swollen eye with, for him, amazing good grace.

"Where'd that kid go?" he asked, looking around. "He has a terrific right cross. I'd like to shake his hand."

"He's up there," Louretta teased, pointing to the ceiling. "With that flock of birds you just heard passing over."

"Aahh," Fess said in disgust. "Women. You don't appreciate the manly art of self-defense." Apparently he did, so much that he was willing to forgive—and respect—anyone who could knock him down twice.

But she replied, "I'd appreciate the fifty cents you owe us."

"Aahh," he complained again. But he paid, with unusual good humor, and stumped over to the piano, where several of the boys were struggling with their new instruments. Mr. Lucitanno had not arrived yet, and Blind Eddie was filling in by giving David a few pointers on his new bass viol. Well, not exactly new—it had a broken string and a finish that was peeling off to show plywood—but it wasn't bad for twenty dollars.

"Now, son, a bass fiddle is like a big, headstrong woman," Blind Eddie explained. "You got to show her you're the boss, or she'll rule you forever. Grab her by the neck, now, and give her a couple of whacks."

David could whack the fiddle, all right, but he couldn't play it. While he demonstrated this fact to everyone's discomfort, Frank produced a few toneless bleats on his new (used) trumpet.

Blind Eddie had to admit that they needed more practice. Fess was much more blunt about it. "You guys sound like a bunch of sick animals," he said. "Why don't you let somebody else have those instruments and stick to what you know already?"

He shuffled restlessly around the piano, making a complete circuit, hands shoved deep in his pockets. Louretta giggled softly. She knew what he was waiting for: He wanted them to perform one of the songs for which he had written lyrics. It was almost as if he had become addicted to hearing them, and had to come around daily for a dose of his personal drug. Once satisfied, he would usually leave, at peace with the world, like any addict after his fix. But he was much too proud to come right out and ask for it. The closest he would come was to hint by whistling one of the tunes, as he was doing now. The tune of "Hungry Cat Blues."

Louretta giggled again. Frank, thinking she was laughing at him, put down his trumpet.

"Gee whiz," he complained, "a guy has to learn *some-time*. Guess I'll have to practice at home for a while. All right, Lou, you win. We'll sing."

She sat down at the piano and rippled the keys softly. To her surprise and delight the notes were clear and harmonious. The piano had been tuned!

She was eager to play it, but Ulysses said, "Don't feel like singing. Don't know any good songs." Then he winked at Louretta and jerked his head toward Fess, who was

228

moodily standing at the far side of the room, looking up at the ceiling with elaborate indifference.

"We've teased him enough," she whispered, and launched into the "Blues." While she played the introduction, she watched Fess's expression relax into a self-satisfied, almost simple-minded smile, and thought how preferable it was to his former sneer. He had been a snarling tiger, but his satisfied vanity had transformed him into a tame pussycat.

He was much more cooperative these days about the newspaper, too. Miss Hodges had agreed, on Louretta's request, to submit materials to Fess for approval, rather than vice versa, since *he* was the editor. Not many teachers would have gone along with a plan like that.

Once Fess had received this concession, he immediately tried to give it back, offering, since he'd done one issue on his own, to let Miss Hodges do the next one. To be equally gracious, she had refused, and they had ended up with neither of them knowing who was really in charge. Louretta didn't know what they were planning to put in the next issue, either, but she knew it would include something about Negro history—probably the history of Negroes and the arts—because she had told Miss Hodges about the day Donna had declared that Louretta's ancestors had never written any poetry.

The teacher had been astonished. "But, Louretta, how could you fall for that? Our people are the most creative group in America. They always have been! Their music, their poetry, their dances . . ."

"I know that now," Louretta said, "because I learned

so much about it from Blind Eddie. But I never learned it in school. How come, Miss Hodges?"

Miss Hodges had looked crestfallen. "I don't know. Maybe somebody wants to keep it a secret."

"Why don't you teach it to us?"

"Dear," Miss Hodges said then, patting her hand, "you must understand something. I have bosses just like everybody else who works, and they tell me what I'm supposed to teach. If I started making up my own courses, I'd be in trouble."

"I mean at the *clubhouse*," Louretta had said patiently. Then she added, "You know, I don't even think Longfellow was such a good poet any more. I think a lot of Blind Eddie's blues lyrics are better."

Miss Hodges considered this for a moment, then said, "I think a lot of people might agree with you, Louretta." Then she came to her decision. "All right. It will take a lot of research—I never had Negro history in school, either—but I'll try. And if I can work up some good lessons, I'll ask Fess to put them in the newspaper."

So that was holding up the next issue of *The Weekly Truth*, which might turn out to be a monthly. As for the first issue, it had been read widely all over the city, with results that Louretta was just beginning to learn about. The huge crowd at the funeral, with its scattering of notables, had been one result. But that was only the beginning.

They were halfway through "Hungry Cat Blues" when three well-dressed men Louretta had never seen before stamped in, shaking the snow from their shoes, blowing frosty air from their lungs, and carrying large, heavy suitcases. Seeing them in this neighborhood was as strange as seeing Polar bears in Africa.

"Three white men just came in," she explained to Blind Eddie, who looked worried.

"You sure this is the right place, Fred?" one of them said.

The oldest and biggest one glanced at a piece of paper. "He said 1343 Lambert Avenue. This is that address." Then he caught sight of the group at the piano. "This is it," he told his companions. "As you were, kids. Don't mind us. Go on with what you were doing."

But Louretta and her friends were much too startled to go on singing.

Fess, annoyed at the interruption, came out of his temporary trance and voiced his worst suspicions.

"Cops!" he cried. "Plainclothes cops! Calvin and I were fighting when she came in, so she called them."

The boys had never forgotten Louretta's threat to scream for the police that night they were planning to riot. Though she had not carried it out, and was not even sure she would have been able to, they would never fully trust her again. Now all of them were looking at her with dark, suspicious eyes.

Then the tall, gray-haired man who seemed to be in charge stepped forward and handed Louretta a card. "We're not police, Miss," he said. "We're friends of your music teacher, Mr. Lucitanno."

She stared at the printed card. It read:

Jewel Records
Every One a Musical Gem
Fred Marcus, Vice-President

"I don't understand," she said, returning the card and lifting her eyes to the big man's friendly gray ones.

"We're from Jewel Records. A recording company. Al Lucitanno thought we ought to listen to your group."

"What for?" David asked belligerently.

"We might want you to record for us," one of the younger men explained.

"Lucitanno was very complimentary," said the other one. "In fact he was so excited after he heard you sing at that funeral, he practically dragged us here the next day. He said you had a unique sound and a great beat. An unusual sound with a good beat, that's what we're looking for."

"Like our other groups, the Fabulettes, the Dacrons, Jimmy Hill and the Climbers . . ." the first one explained.

Louretta was impressed. *All* the kids were impressed. Those were famous names.

"As a matter of fact, I *know* they've got the sound," Mr. Marcus said. "I caught a few bars on TV. Only the finish, but *what* a finish! I hope no one else has been here to sign them up."

Louretta shook her head. "You mean we were on TV?" she asked incredulously.

"Yes, on the evening news. They showed a few clips of the funeral. And, by the way, congratulations."

"What for?" Louretta wanted to know.

"You should watch television more often, young lady," the vice-president reproved her. "They suspended the cop that shot your friend. And that lieutenant, what's-his-name, was transferred to another district."

"Lafferty?" Fess said incredulously.

"That's the one. It was all on account of a sheet some kids got up and printed. It aroused a lot of feeling in the community."

The group cheered, whistling and stamping their feet, and Fess began to puff up with pride. But they soon became silent, and more than a little scared, watching the men unpack their suitcases to reveal an awesome collection of recording equipment.

Blind Eddie, who could not see the dazzling display of microphones and tape recorders, was not bashful, however. "I used to record on the Jewel label," he said. "Twenty years ago, when I was with Erskine Hawkins. And before that, too."

The gray-haired vice-president bent and inspected Eddie's face. "My God! It's Blind Eddie Bell!" he exclaimed. "I didn't think he was still around. A great guitarist, boys," he explained to his assistants. "A little before your time, though. You're too young to remember him."

He shook Eddie's hand and reintroduced himself. "Fred Marcus, Eddie. It's great to see you again."

The old musician's face was illuminated with a happy smile. "Oh, I remember you. Little Fred. You were just a young sprout back then. Fresh out of college."

"Yes, well, I'm completely gray now," the younger man said. "So are you, I see. But you seem to be holding up fine, Eddie."

"Oh, I get along," Eddie said, beaming. "Fooling around with these young people keeps me young. But it sure is good to meet an old friend."

"What have you got to be so happy about, old man?" Fess demanded, baring his teeth and snarling like his old self. "Do you know how he earns his living now? *Begging!*" he told the white men, then turned back to Eddie. "With all your talent, you should be rich. Instead, these no-talent guys have been getting rich off your records. They're all dressed up in silk suits, and you're wearing rags."

Blind Eddie was unruffled. "That's true," he admitted, "but they ain't never had the pleasure of playing and writing music. That's worth more to me than money."

"Aaaahh," Fess exploded in disgust. "That's the kind of backward thinking that keeps us in slavery."

The executive had been embarrassed for a moment, but now he recovered his poise, and said firmly to Fess, "Blind Eddie's been neglected by the new generation, son. It's people *your* age who buy records, and they don't seem to dig him like their parents did. So if he's poor, it's not our fault. It's yours. But maybe we can do something about it."

Turning his attention back to Eddie, he said more gently, "So you've been coaching these teen-agers, huh, Eddie?"

"Oh, just a little bit," Blind Eddie said modestly. "They don't need much coaching. They're pretty good on their own."

"Fellows," the executive said dramatically, turning to his companions, "I think we may have a find. A young group coached by an old-time genius." He seemed excited as he gave directions. "Kids, if you will, please run through the number you did at the church. The one about the boy who died."

" 'Lament for Jethro,' " Louretta supplied.

"Great title," one of the younger men said appreciatively.

"Pretend we're not here," Marcus said encouragingly. "Just go ahead and sing the way you do when you're alone."

Noticing Louretta's apprehensive glance at the equipment, which included three tape recorders, all spinning, he explained, "Oh, this is just a trial tape to see how you sound. We're not recording now."

She moved aside to let Blind Eddie play the piano, but when she nudged him toward it, the old man refused. "No, little girl," he said. "You know the piano part by now. You don't need my help any more. You can do it on your own."

Panicking, she pleaded with him, but he refused to yield. Finally, feeling numb, she sat down and struck the first stately chords. They were rich and clear; the newly tuned piano had a good tone. She knew she had Mr. Lucitanno to thank for that.

Then the boys' voices came in, firm and strong, all around her. They were off and swinging, the piano cooperating beautifully like the thoroughbred old Baptist-church piano it was, Louretta singing in her deepest, most somber voice, which was half alto, half tenor, and sounded like a mature woman's. She put everything she could remember of the funeral into it—the tears of the mourners, Reverend Mamie's impassioned preaching, the congregation's emotional responses—and everything she could remember of Jethro, and all of herself.

When it was over, there was a long silence. Then one of the technicians shut off his tape recorder with a one-word comment:

"Wow."

"What d'you call that sound, chief?" the other one asked. "It's not exactly pop, and not exactly blues either. It has an almost—*religious* flavor."

Fess provided the one-word answer:

"Soul."

Louretta, warmed by his highest word of praise, felt grateful tears rise in her eyes. Now she knew what this quality was that he prized so highly, and also knew that she possessed it. It came out in her singing and playing, but music was only one way of expressing it. Soul was in Ulysses' laughter, too, and in Momma's crying, and Reverend Mamie's preaching, as well as in Mrs. Jackson's dancing and Randolph's smiles. It was a way of putting your whole self, your deepest self, into everything you did. It meant having feelings in such a way that all of you was involved. Not just your head, but your body too—which was why the people at the Baptist church patted their feet and clapped their hands and danced in the aisles at services, and why nearly all the colored people she had ever seen used their whole bodies in talking, their arms and heads and shoulders and hips and knees, not just their mouths. They all had this way of putting themselves completely into everything they did, and so did Louretta. She was not different from the soul people at all; she was one of them.

Blind Eddie spoke up. "You have to suffer a little to have soul. You have to live a little while."

Maybe that was what had made the difference. In the past few months, she had seen Jethro shot down, her friends turn mutinous, her family threatened with the loss of its security. She had lived "a little while" in that short time, and suffered a good deal.

The vice-president had made a quick decision. "We'll cut that one," he announced. "It's a winner. It's an original, too, isn't it?"

"Yes," Louretta said proudly. "Fess, over there, wrote the words, and Blind Eddie set it to music."

"I thought I recognized a master's touch," Mr. Marcus said.

Louretta was amused to see Fess smile from ear to ear, thinking the man had meant *him*. But his pride was pardonable, and she decided to swell it even further. "He wrote the words to the one we were singing when you came in, too."

"And she set *that* one to music. All by herself," Blind Eddie lied.

"Think you could run through it for us?" Mr. Marcus asked eagerly.

The group was warmed up now, and in top form, having lost all self-consciousness. They performed "Hungry Cat Blues" with spirit and enthusiasm and without a single mistake.

"Folks, I think we've got our record," the recording-company vice-president announced. "We'll put that one on the flip side. All we have to do is set a date for the recording session. Early next week." He pulled out a pocket calendar. "How about Wednesday afternoon?"

Fess was quick to assume the authority which he loved. "Do they get paid?" he demanded. "I'm their manager."

"Of course," the big man answered, with a slight

smile that betrayed his amusement. "We'll work out liberal contracts for all of you. You can submit them to a lawyer if you wish, but I think you'll be satisfied. There will be a nice little sum in advance for each of you, and more if the record is a success. That's all for now, kids. Except, remember to rehearse every day. And start working up some new numbers, too. Especially the poet. We can't do much without *him*."

Fess was glowing with importance. His face was lit from within as if by a candle.

At the door, Mr. Marcus turned. "Oh, one thing more," he said. "Have you thought of a name for your group?"

Fess seized this responsibility, too. "The Soul Brothers," he replied instantly.

"Great," one of the technicians approved.

"Yes, but one of them is a girl," objected the other.

William, who had been listening quietly in the background, stepped forward to supply a solution.

"How about 'The Soul Brothers and Sister Lou'?" he said.

His suggestion met with instant, enthusiastic approval from everyone in the room.

SEVENTEEN

SIX MONTHS HAD GONE BY, AND WHEN LOURETTA LOOKED BACK
at all that had happened, she might believe it had all been a
dream, except that she had two proofs that it was not. One
was her new self, confident and assured, glad to be Louretta Hawkins and no one else, though she had found out
that when you got on the Inside, where she was now,
everything there was not as wonderful as Outsiders supposed. Insiders had *their* problems too.

Her other proof, mounted prominently on the living
room wall at home, was a small, shiny black disc with a
round, red label she knew by heart:

LAMENT FOR JETHRO
(Philip Satterthwaite and Blind Eddie Bell)
THE SOUL BROTHERS AND SISTER LOU
(David Weldon, Frank Brown, Ulysses
McCracken, Louretta Hawkins)

Its other side read:

HUNGRY CAT BLUES
(Philip Satterthwaite and Louretta Hawkins.
Arranger: Blind Eddie Bell)

THE SOUL BROTHERS AND SISTER LOU
(David Weldon, Frank Brown,
Ulysses McCracken, Louretta Hawkins)

The record was surrounded by a display of clippings that covered the entire wall. Louretta hated them and wished Momma would take them down. They reminded her too much of the things that had happened to change her.

First the recording session at the studio, a small, equipment-cluttered room in a low cinder-block building that resembled a garage, but had seemed glamorous as a palace to all of them.

Then the signing of the contracts and the handing out of checks to everyone, including Fess and Blind Eddie. The checks were small in comparison to what they had earned since, but hers had seemed like a fortune to her then. It still did, because she was not allowed to handle any more of her money; none of them were, except Blind Eddie, because they were all under twenty-one. William banked hers for her, kept careful accounts, and gave her a small allowance.

But the first glorious check had been all hers to spend as she pleased, and it had probably given her more pleasure than any money ever would again. She had bought a shiny new washer and dryer for Momma, to end those constant trips to the laundromat, and a bright red winter coat for herself with a dress and hat to match. That purchase was the beginning of her new, confident personality. Now people could call her "Red" all they wanted, and they would have good reason.

She had also sent Arneatha, whose second post card

had said that she was broke and stranded in California, the fare to come home. Not plane fare—there wasn't enough money left for that—but enough for a bus ticket and meals.

It had been interesting to see what the others did with the money they were allowed to spend.

David had immediately bought a bright red motor scooter, and could be seen zipping about the streets at all hours, his head encased in a matching red helmet, his long legs and arms sticking out dangerously into the traffic. All the other girls were eager to ride behind him, but Louretta, after one hair-raising sample, refused. With his habit of cutting in and out of lanes at high speed, it was a miracle that David had had no accidents so far.

Ulysses became a food fiend, and quickly went from a big, husky boy to a big, fat one. Deciding that his athletic days were over, he visited every first-class restaurant in the city and treated himself to the most expensive item on each menu. But soon their fare did not satisfy him, and he began poring over cookbooks and visiting markets all over town —in Little Italy, in Chinatown, in the Greek section, even in the upper-class neighborhoods, which had places called "gourmet shops." He announced his plan to become a chef and open the city's finest restaurant. Louretta had no doubt that he would do just that someday.

In the meantime, each week Ulysses discovered a new recipe or a new delicacy, cooked it, and invited his friends over to dinner. Louretta had refused his latest series of invitations because Ulysses was in what she called his Slimy Period. He had just discovered eel, snails and squid, and the thought of eating such things made her squeamish. Some-day, she hoped, he would return to the kind of good, substantial cooking he had been raised on—Momma's kind of cooking, which was known as "soul food"—and when that happened, Louretta would be one of his steadiest customers.

The transformation of Fess was the most striking of all. Not that his personality had become any less arrogant or that he had gotten any better-looking. No, Louretta was forced to admit that Fess would get no taller and would resemble a dark, pop-eyed frog all his life. Nor had he acquired any expensive habits—he was saving every cent for college. It was just that a little success had been enough to turn Fess completely around. From an ardent revolutionary, he had become an enthusiastic booster of business, free enterprise and capitalism. He was, of course, just as irritatingly dogmatic and dictatorial about his new enthusiasm as he had been about his previous ideas.

He spent long hours arguing with Frank, who had absorbed his leader's earlier theories only too well and wanted to use *his* earnings to buy guns for a revolution.

"No, no, you got the wrong idea, man," Fess would say. "A hundred thousand invested at six per cent a year will get you more power than all the guns in the world."

"No, man, we can't join these people. We gotta *fight* 'em," Frank would insist stubbornly.

"Well, what are you gonna have when you *finish* fighting?"

It was unanswerable. Frank continued to resist Fess's arguments. He still spent all his spare hours studying rifle manuals and catalogs. But one day he suddenly got up, went downtown, and bought a red scooter exactly like David's.

242

Frank really had no immediate use for a gun—none of them did—because the Hawks were no more. Their enemies, the Avengers, who had been the main reason for the Hawks' existence, had become their closest associates, dropping around daily at the clubhouse which Blind Eddie had refurbished with his royalties.

Everyone had tried to talk Blind Eddie out of it, but the old man was determined to be generous. "Only thing I might buy for myself is a guitar," he said, "and I wouldn't play it anyway. I'm too attached to this old one. She's been with me for forty years."

When they said, "What about your family?", he replied, "I ain't got no family. You're my family, and this place is my home."

To those who exhorted Blind Eddie to save his money for his old age, he said, "I've already *had* my old age. This is my second childhood."

So he had his way, and, with a separate entrance and a sign dedicating it to Jethro, the clubhouse now occupied the second floor of William's building, and included three splendid rooms: a print shop in the back, with its own small press and mimeograph machine and a drafting table for Calvin; a music room in the middle, with a new tape recorder and the old piano which Louretta had insisted on keeping; and a large lounge in front, with TV, records, snack machines, a sofa and comfortable chairs. Handrails for Blind Eddie ran up the stairs and around all the walls, because the old man was there constantly. He even slept there.

William now had the entire first floor for his growing, full-time business. The kids never intruded there except for special events—large public meetings and dances which were always held at night.

The place had everything Louretta and her friends could possibly want now—privacy, a resident watchman, even the reluctant tolerance of the police. But The Soul Brothers and Sister Lou seldom went there, except to work on songs, and for that they picked hours when no one else was around. The clubhouse had become a hangout for kids, and they were kids no longer.

Louretta was glad that Andrew and the others his age had a place to go besides the street corners and something to do besides fighting in gangs. But she was sorry that she and her companions had grown up so fast. Their new life had made that inevitable, though.

A few weeks after the recording session, when their money had been spent and they were beginning to believe it had all been a dream, a popular local disc jockey, known as "Big Mouth" for his loud and incessant patter, had started playing their record on his show, and talking about it whenever he wasn't playing it.

The other disc jockeys began getting requests for the record, the word got around, and "Lament for Jethro" began to be played on radio stations all around the country and to appear on jukeboxes everywhere.

It was a hit—and Arneatha came home to find that it was her little sister who had become the star.

The effect of this on Arneatha was probably the thing that had saddened Louretta most. Whatever Arneatha's dreams had been, they had been smashed in Hollywood. No one had noticed her there; she had been unable to get even a waitress job, and finally, broke and hungry, had been evicted from her room for nonpayment of rent. Now she seemed to have given up. She no longer cared about makeup and clothes, though Louretta offered to buy her some, and since her former boy friends had lost interest in her, she never went out. Instead, she drifted around the house like a ghost, dressed in shabby slacks and housedresses, and clinging to Cora Lee as if the baby were all she had left.

But Cora Lee, not knowing who this strange, nervous woman was, cried to be put down when Arneatha held her, and ran to Louretta or Momma instead. Louretta and her mother tried to train the little girl to go to her real mother for her needs. But their efforts met with little success. Arneatha and her baby had been strangers for too long.

When she realized that Cora Lee would not accept her as her mother, Arneatha gave up completely and spent most of her time upstairs, crying in her room. Then one night she attempted to slash her wrists with a razor in order to bleed to death, and had to be taken to a hospital. She was still there, with what was called a "nervous breakdown." But Louretta called it a case of giving up.

Meanwhile, Big Mouth, who in private was soft-spoken and polite, had the four on his radio program and arranged a series of appearances for them at jazz shows, record hops, school assemblies and dances. Scared at first, they changed quickly from shy, awkward amateurs to poised professionals, accustomed to singing before audiences and even able to speak to groups about their experiences. Then the late hours and the excitement began to interfere with sleep and schoolwork, and Momma put her foot down. But not before they had become celebrities,

245

objects of the awe and envy of their classmates, and no longer ordinary students at Southern High. Joella Evans was now not the only schoolmate who resented Louretta. Her scheme to acquire a circle of friends had been so successful it left her lonelier than ever.

At the beginning, whenever Louretta came home from an appearance, Momma went to work with a rough washrag to remove every trace of her makeup. And then she would hide it, along with her daring black dress and her first pair of high-heeled shoes. Louretta resented this bitterly at the time, not understanding what Momma was trying to do until it was too late. She was trying to prevent Louretta from growing up too fast. But in spite of her efforts, it had happened—a growing up that was not a matter of clothing and makeup but had taken place inside.

The joy of discovering inspiring poetry and exciting historic heroes at school was gone, because she would never quite believe in those mottoes and heroes again. The thrill of spending the first money she had ever earned had changed to a dull routine of inspecting account books with long rows of meaningless figures, and cosigning checks with William to pay inexplicable bills. The excitement of improvising the first songs and making the first recording had become the hard work of rehearsing and perfecting numbers for the second. It got tougher, not easier; the Jewel Records people and the agent the four had inevitably acquired kept urging them to achieve a unique style and stick to it, and to beware of their competition, lest they become has-beens at seventeen. Music had been a childhood pleasure to Louretta, but now it was work. It was good to have money in the bank and fun to see your picture in the papers once or twice, but you soon got used to these things, and it had been more fun to get together with a bunch of kids and sing the way you wanted in an alley or a shabby room.

Louretta didn't know what she had gained that was worth giving that up. There was the money, of course, but she couldn't touch it—and even when she could, what would she spend it on? Momma and William had investigated the possibility of a new house, but had found nothing available for colored families as large as theirs in better neighborhoods. After many refusals and bitter disappointments, they had decided to stay where they were.

Money could send her to college, of course, but now that money was no problem, she was no longer sure she wanted to go. In fact, she was no longer sure about anything—not even Calvin, who had become her constant companion.

He made so many remarks about her new wealth that she was beginning to suspect him of being a mite jealous. And a romance with a jealous boy was bound to turn bitter. Louretta knew all the reasons why boys of her race had more problems than girls, and she was already beginning to wonder if this would happen to her all her life with men who were less successful than she. Sometimes Calvin said it humorously, sometimes angrily, and sometimes wistfully, but he never failed to bring up her success whenever he was with her, and she was becoming increasingly irritable about it.

Tonight, as usual, he said, "How's the little rich gal?" when he dropped in for his nightly coffee and dessert with Louretta and Momma. It was a point of pride with him to bring the dessert—usually a pie or cake from the restaurant, but tonight, ice cream.

Feeling unusually sensitive, she took out the allowance she had just been given and flung it on the table.

"You can have it, if you want. What good is it, anyway? It won't bring Jethro back."

But what she meant was: *It won't bring the old days back. Not mine, not his, and not yours.* The old days, when all of them could be silly, the way Jethro had been, silly and crazy and gay, and get away with it. Only, Jethro *hadn't* gotten away with it.

A tear fell on the pile of bills. Then Calvin picked up the money, folded it into her hand with a squeeze, and said something so wise and understanding she began to believe they might remain friends after all.

"Enjoy what you have now, Louretta. Nothing ever comes back," he said.